THE
ORPHANARIUM

S.T.
CARTLEDGE

ERASERHEAD PRESS
PORTLAND, OREGON

ERASERHEAD PRESS
PO BOX 10065
PORTLAND, OR 97296

WWW.ERASERHEADPRESS.COM

ISBN: 978-1-62105-245-6

Copyright © 2017 by S.T. Cartledge

"Overgrown" was originally published in the anthology *Wishing Weird* (Fireside Press, 2016).

Cover art copyright © 2017 by Hauke Vagt

Printed in the USA.

AUTHOR'S NOTE

I need to thank Dr. Deborah Hunn for this book. The first section came together after careful writing and plotting and editing over days and weeks and months as I pieced it together alongside the exegesis which would form my honours dissertation.

I need to thank Cameron Pierce, for helping me to find its home with Eraserhead Press. I need to thank Spike Marlowe too for being my editor at Eraserhead while I bounced countless ideas off her because even though we didn't publish anything together, those messages and emails were an important step in getting me here. I need to thank Rose O'Keefe, for being pure magic. She edited this book something fierce.

I need to thank my writing friends, who are too many to count. I'd start with Michael Allen Rose, Kirk Jones, Gabino Iglesias, Joseph Bouthiette Jr., Karl Fischer, Vincenzo Bilof. William Pauley III, G Arthur Brown. Vince Kramer. The Bizarro family, the Bizarro fans. The list goes on. My poetry friends, because this thing started as a poem. If it weren't for poetry, this book wouldn't exist.

I need to list the specific sources of inspiration which compelled me to write this thing: Richard Brautigan's In Watermelon Sugar, Akira (both the manga and the anime), Ghost in the Shell (both the manga and anime), Serial Experiments Lain, Neon Genesis Evangelion, Kaiba, Nausicaa of the Valley of the Wind (the Miyazaki manga), Howl's Moving Castle (the Miyazaki film), William Gibson's Neuromancer, Neil Gaiman's American Gods, China Mieville's Kraken. Everything by Tsutomu Nihei, and in particular his debut manga series Blame!

This book is my love song to Nihei, and to the Bizarro dystopian landscapes carved out by some of my literary heroes like Carlton Mellick III, Cameron Pierce, and D. Harlan Wilson.

I need to thank you for taking a risk on me with this one. Hold on to my cactus-exploded heart. I hope you love every minute of this.

"In watermelon sugar, the deeds were done and done again, as my life is done in watermelon sugar."

—Richard Brautigan, *In Watermelon Sugar* (1968)

INSIDE

CHAPTER X

This book is full of variables. Some things we know. Some things we don't know. Some things we're going to find out when the time is right. Some of it just comes down to how well we know the details. How we process the information.

We don't know it yet, but Cyberia will be the first of us to die.

CHAPTER ZERO

Exposition:

Here is us. We are here in the Orphanarium. Think: A city in a massive box. Vacuum sealed tight like no one would be allowed outside. No one is allowed outside. Here, people are born out of the air or made like computers and put together. And we are in the farming sector outside of district AKO with the sun-globes tracking overhead on steel cables and the honey tinted air hanging low and thick in a field of candylions.

Who we are:

Daff is me and Dil is you and together we are twins pulled from the same vacuum of space. Cyberia is our friend android and she has a window in her head, a sphere like a crystal mind monitor. Our pet is called Killy, a cyborg dog who was born out of the air like you and me, but has since been built up with robot parts so she can live longer. Some people do that around here too – some people want to live forever – but you know how it is. You know all of this already. Say hello to your future self reading this.

Yeah, this is the way things are. And the way things are right now is all about the situation with the Elementals. Some people are calling it a war. For others, it's more of a slaughter. Us or them, it's never specified. But there's always talk of what's going on outside the Orphanarium. Whispers of what's happening out there. Truth is we don't know until we find out. And we won't find out while we're over here surrounded by candylions grazing on their holographic grass.

Let this world dissolve around you. Seal it in a distant sector in your mind.

DREAM CHAPTER IN THE NIGHT SECTOR
(OR CHAPTER OF A MEMORY YET TO COME)

There is a hyper-saturation of tinting in the air. Violet. The night sector in MLO with the sprawling towers twisting into spires like giant conical shells. Conveyor belts pass from tower to tower; thousands of silver tokens on the silent belts, sleeping. The floor is a black silicon grid and it absorbs my footsteps and Killy's and it feels like we are ghosts in this place. This side of the Orphanarium is where people go for rest, for recharging, for retirement. There is a whole other city on this side for the night walkers, for the people that come here and don't want to go back. For us day dwellers, we have no need for the night sector while we are so young. The soft glowing night-lights track along the roof, casting their dim lights on this land. Everyone who is asleep right now is transformed and compressed into little silver coins, sleep tokens, and they come out the other side re-orphaned and refreshed. I've been dropped in this place and it's kind of hard to breathe and at the same time I'm experiencing this moment from the past in a dream, a memory from the World Cactus. Be patient, everything will come to light.

I'm dreaming this and you're dreaming something else and Cyberia is dreaming something else entirely. All around the World Cactus dreaming. And the cool air on my skin in the night sector is trying to push me to the towers and compress me into a token. The dim moon lights cast monolithic shadows of the towers onto the ground. Shadows that can't be seen but are felt just as dark and heavy as though they could. One of these shadows rolls over me and my bones rattle as it tries to transform me into a token and put me to sleep.

I'm not going to sleep here. The coins in the towers and on the conveyor belts are restless. The air is quivering and the coins are shivering like something big is coming, feels like an earthquake. They're shivering and the sound of coin rattling on coin is muted, absorbed into the night sector air.

From the air comes a low, wailing siren, a loud 'wub-wub-wub-wub' noise, and the Jingo Monitor lizards are in here firing their light beams about wildly at the tokens that have been awakened back to their material selves. And the light beams trap all of us from going anywhere. Hung in their bright lights, we hear whispered rumours that an Elemental has entered the Orphanarium. The rumours say it was in district SEL. But Jingo don't play with rumours. And they don't want us running around panicking or trying to hunt the creature down. They just want to return us to tokens and return us to sleep. The Monitors turn the alarm off and lighten the tinting in the night sector. Then they slink back into the shadows with a lick of their lizard tongues and a shift of their lizard tails. In the instant the last Monitor turns its light off, there is the frame of a young girl carved out of light. Her vanishing eyes catch mine, and then I am back with you and Cyberia and the World Cactus.

In this moment, I don't know what I am doing there. Or why I am wandering the night sector when the alarm goes off, when the Jingo arrive. Or what that part at the end is with the girl in the light. Her name is Sunburst, and that fleeting image of her face burned into my eyes is what you might call a destiny. I will meet her again later and find out her name, but right now, I am awakened from my coma as you are from yours and Cyberia from hers. Killy is not here, because of her fear of elevators. We are at the World Cactus with bloody spines sticking in our palms. And just as Cyberia has died/is dying/will die, none of us know what we're doing now is an act of war.

CHAPTER WHERE WE RIDE THE ELEVATOR

There is Cyberia holding the hands of you and me and the glass window in her skull shines bright. Her window flickers and the maintenance elevator rumbles into operation and takes us to a place that people and cyborgs and androids are not supposed to go. And Cyberia, she's a technomancer. A special breed of android that can get us there. She speaks the silent language of machines. She can access data and manipulate it in countless ways we could never dream.

"I been here loads of times before," she says. "You're going to love it."

In the elevator, the air is tinted black and on the wall there is the orange reptile logo and the words "Jingo Incorporated". The faded paint is the hue of old rust, and it appears that something wet has trickled down the walls and started rusting out the rest of it.

She is bouncing on the balls of her feet. Today her eyes are green, her lips are pale green, and her hair is a slightly darker shade of green, with her fibre-optic bangs framed around her glass window. And those flashes of colour contrast the paleness in the rest of her face. Her hands are cold.

The elevator ride lasts fifteen, maybe twenty minutes. Each minute passing in silence. Each minute going faster and faster as the light in the crack of the door falls down with each level we ascend. An exponential guillotine. It feels like she's going to kill us. We'd hit the roof so hard we'd break right through, if only we knew how high the roof is. If there is a roof. The floors guillotine down, shun, shun, shun. Her hands wind tighter into ours, and her window shines brighter and lifts the tinting in the air. The walls are coded with black paint, secret guerrilla messages, beginning with "FUCKING JINGO SCUM" and trailing down the walls in a back-and-forth exchange until "Meet me at the crossroads outside TNX noon tomorrow."

The light in Cyberia's head goes out and there is just the dull orange on the wall and the slowing light-guillotine, until it hits the right floor and stops and opens. Cyberia opens her mouth and says, "We're here."

She takes you and me by the hand into a massive wide room with a pale green tinting in the air. There are vines and creepers growing on the walls and hanging hundreds of metres from the ceiling. There are about a dozen suns tracking their way across the ceiling and making grinding gear noises in their slow revolutions.

"Cool," you say.

"There's more," Cyberia says. "There's something here I want to show you."

She disappears around a giant fern, following a path through the growth, and we vanish into the room after her.

"How did you find this place?" you ask.

She looks back and says, "I don't remember. I guess you could say that it found me."

We step over a creek that runs into the wall, and we can see little glowing fish in the water.

"Not much further," Cyberia says.

A tree that looks like a dragon wraps itself around a concrete beam. Limbs twisting and stretching and splitting and going insane. Up ahead the wilderness recedes. Up ahead there is a statue of a cactus, tall and thin. And there are people crowded around it.

"Is that it?" you say.

Cyberia nods.

"Who are those people?"

"That's us," she says. "By the World Cactus."

"What?"

She smiles. "I've been waiting for this day for a long time, to share the cactus with you."

"How are *we-*" your hand circles us, "-over *there?*" You point to the others.

"The cactus exists in a time vacuum. It is always there and it always will be there. Just as we are there once, we are forever standing around the World Cactus. Come. Let me show you."

She takes our hands again and leads us over to the World Cactus.

CACTUS CHAPTER ONE

There we are, beside each other, duplicated as a hologram around the World Cactus. Our hologram selves are slumped on the ground, bodies limp but our eyelids are flickering like we're processing thought, like we're seeing something in there.

Cyberia walks up to the base of the cactus, ignoring the duplicates.

"What you do, is you get one of the spines," she says, plucking spines from the cactus, "And stab it in you." She takes my hand and brings a razor-sharp, bone-white spine right up to it. "Like this. And you see bits and pieces from your life."

Stab.

Exactly like that. She does the same for you. Blood dribbles down our palms, down our wrists onto her fingers. Her cold fingers. Do you think her hands are cold because there's no blood left in them?

"One spine, one memory," Cyberia says.

The World Cactus is big and blue and twisted and gnarled. It shows us our memories from the end of time. They may have already happened, but because we are relatively young and because we will likely live for a very long time, the World Cactus will most likely show us future memories. Cyberia pushes on her breastplate and a compartment pops open. There are bloody spines filling it, her collected memories clumped together like a splintered explosion of her robot heart.

She's a cactus junkie.

Your face is shiny from sweat. A layer of glass covers you, Dil. In this moment, you're nowhere real. In this moment, everything around me dissolves.

PLANT-BOY CHAPTER

He wears a crown of burning roses. The roses don't shrivel or wilt, and the flames don't extinguish. The creature I can only call 'Plant-Boy' comes out of the sky with a crack and lands like a torpedo. The spines on the World Cactus rattle and fall to the dirt.

"You will not be dreaming the cactus dreams any more," Plant-Boy says.

"No," Cyberia says. "This is not how the memory goes."

"You will leave this place and never come back."

"This is *not* how the memory goes," Cyberia says.

"I know how the memory goes."

"Who are you? And where did you come from?" she grabs Plant-Boy, her skull-window flickering like mad.

Plant-Boy shoots ectoplasm at Cyberia's face.

"Leave!" he roars, and sets fire to the cactus.

Cyberia grabs and scratches at the ectoplasm. She tries to breathe, but can't. She falls over and wrestles with her Plant-Boy face mask.

Plant-Boy waits for Cyberia to run out of energy before kneeling down beside her. "You saw what you saw because I wanted you to see it," he says. "You do not want the Jingo to find you here. There are so many things the spines don't tell you."

Plant-Boy takes a small bottle from his pocket and drizzles it delicately over Cyberia's face. It sizzles and cracks the ectoplasm. He turns and runs straight into the burning cactus. In a whoosh, he is gone.

CHAPTER OF STEALING CYBERIA'S SPINES

Cyberia is motionless on the ground. Carbon-fiber chest rising and falling slowly. The charcoal husk of the burnt-out World Cactus glowing purple/red. Needle seeds scattered at its base. Needle seeds scattered by Cyberia, her chest cavity tumbled to the ground. Her spine-cluster heart burst apart by the air.

"One spine, one memory," she says/has said/will say.

Her used memories.

You pick up a spine and say, "how long has Cyberia been living in her dreams?"

I shrug. Your guess is as good as mine. Still sticking out of my palm is the spine that had me dreaming of the Night Sector, and the girl called Sunburst. I pull it out, the bloody tip, a dark brown/purple ring remaining on my skin. With the removal comes a longing to revisit the memory, to see Sunburst again, to dwell in the Night Sector memory for another time. Possibly scanning for clues as to exactly when this event will take place. Hoping that it wasn't fabricated or distorted like what Plant-Boy did to Cyberia.

You have already placed Cyberia's second-hand memory spine into your palm-hole and invaded her dream. This may be the only chance we get to see inside her head. I pocket my spine and grab one of hers and slide it into my skin.

Dissolution again. A cold, wet sensation melting from the top of my head down. You and Cyberia and the smouldering cactus are gone, gone, gone. I am Cyberia's memory. In her body, through her android eyes I see. And through the window in her head I filter and process the world's programs that occur around me. At the molecular level, the texture of the ground is slick. The surface constantly changing state: evaporative. Smelling like thousands of years of giant engines in constant motion. Cool air is wide open, perhaps a billion cubic meters around us. Air particles vibrating, the song of machines in motion, and the distant grinding gears and tracks of the many slowly moving suns far above us.

This is the brief moment before my (Cyberia's) termination. Cyberia is dead and the memory ends. So much more happened right there than my organic brain could take in. I saw the killer's face, yet recall nothing.

Cyberia is awake. Her cold hands grip me by the ankles. Your hands carry my wrists.

How long was I out for, Dil? Do you remember?

No, I don't suppose you would.

"He's awake," you say.

"Good. We can set him down," Cyberia says.

"Hey buddy," you say. "You doing ok?"

I nod.

"We need to get out of here, Daff. The Jingo are coming."

CRACK IN THE WALL AND LOCKDOWN CHAPTER

We disappear further into the room, the glowing cactus shrinking away from us. The logic behind this is that if we went back the way we came we would run into the Jingo and they would obliterate us. We need to make our own exits.

Cyberia walks ahead of you and me and for a while she doesn't say anything about what just happened at the World Cactus. Then:

"Which memories did you see?" She is real quiet asking this.

"We were all outside," you say. "It was freezing, and there were these big strange demons wandering around."

"They're called Elementals," Cyberia says.

"They hurt my head."

"What about you, Daff? What did you see?"

I tilt my head down and keep walking. Image of Cyberia dying, burned into my eyes.

"Don't touch my memories again," she says.

I nod and you nod and we reach the other end of the room and the wall shimmers like a hologram. Cyberia touches the wall. Her light-window flashes white and there is a thunder crack and all the light in the room vanishes.

Dull red glow from the cactus.

"Cyberia, are you ok?" you ask her.

She isn't responding.

"Cyberia."

Nothing.

Meanwhile, on the other side of the room:

Torchlight beams cut through the dark air and stick to the pale green tinting. The Jingo Monitor lizards are coming. The Orphanarium will no doubt go into lockdown.

"We need to leave," you say. "Now. Grab Cyberia's feet."

I don't know where you're planning on going, but you do. Like perhaps you remember it happening already. A light beam swings across the wall and passes over a place high up and right above where we are now. A crack in the wall that turns into a small hole right about where Cyberia touched it. A small hole through which to crawl. Strange things are happening here and I'm not sure who is behind it all.

SUNBURST
CHAPTER ONE

Girl on fire. Behind the wall in the crawlspace there is the girl on fire. From my memory in the Night Sector, she is the one I will come to know as Sunburst. She was born out of a dead star, her father who released his energy and then became nothing. She is like Plant-Boy and the World Cactus in that she isn't from here and she doesn't belong. We have Cyberia slumped against the wall inside the crawlspace. We are hiding out in this pocket of damp air; the tinting is thick black like tar, and we're waiting for her to come back around. This is when the girl on fire appears to us, a light in the dark crawlspace. We are unsure if she is coming closer or moving away. We watch her, then chase after her, yet her light flickers further away as if we must follow it.

I love her.

CHAPTER WHERE YOU LEAVE US FOR THE WAR

You drape Cyberia's arms over your shoulders and tuck her legs around your waist. We follow the glowing light of Sunburst like our lives depend on it, but we're doing it for different reasons. The crawlspace is narrow and tall and straight and toxic. We walk for I don't know how long, and when you get tired of carrying Cyberia, I carry her, and when I get tired, you carry her. When we both get tired, we stop for a minute to rest. The light of my love only has one path to follow. I am confident we will not lose her and that she will not disappear.

Cyberia wakes with a flicker and a hum. Her programs restarting.

We can't see Sunburst any more. She is too far ahead or she has disappeared. Maybe she is a holographic projection of Cyberia's subconscious programming.

We continue along the crawlspace to the spot where we last saw Sunburst. In the dark it should be hard to see, but it isn't. You and I can both sense it, and Cyberia senses it too. There is a hole in the wall where the tar-like tinting is leaking out. A breeze flows into the crawlspace and it feels like nothing I've ever felt in the Orphanarium before. It pulls at us and sucks us through to the other side of the wall.

We are outside everything.

"This is my memory," you yell over the violent wind. "Coming outside."

We are on a little ledge with no barrier. There is wall stretching either side as far as we can see and there is no floor and no ceiling. Way up there is sky and way down there is ground. Or earth. Or whatever it's called that's beneath the floor that continues everywhere.

Sunburst is gone.

There is no tinting in the air. And your voice is whipped around by the wind. "I'm leaving," you yell.

"You can't," Cyberia replies. "You can't."

"I have to. My future is out here."

"It doesn't have to be," she says. "It doesn't have to be your war."

You shrug. "If I don't do it, who will?" You slide off the ledge and drop down the wall. The wind throws you against the wall with raw Elemental power.

Your war has already begun.

CACTUS CHAPTER TWO

Cyberia and I, we're standing out here on the edge of everything. Out here is where no-one goes. There is just red sand and dead trees beyond. The sky is dark blue, penetrated by a single silver moon sitting in the sky like a full-stop but reading more like a question mark hanging out over everything that's never been seen.

This part of the story is for you. Everything you're not around to witness while you're off fighting your war.

Killy transports herself into Cyberia's arms. She moves through the circuits of the city, visible and invisible, through air and walls, disassembling and reassembling and downloading her personality and memory data from the network. She barks three times. A warning.

Killy came to us because the Jingo found our crawlspace. They're coming for us, and you're too busy fighting the wind to come back. If you see Sunburst, send her our way. Cyberia and I aren't fit for the outside world. We can't fight the Elementals. We're not brave like you.

And the Cactus is gone. All that remains are the spines it gave us. They've done nothing but terrorise us. Cyberia is sick. She is weak with cactus fever. She is mad. She told us this World Cactus would be here forever but it's already dead. And the Jingo are so eager to hunt us down and once they are done killing us they will seal this city back up again like a vacuum. They can not lose control of the city. That's why they're fighting the Elementals. That's why we can't go outside.

CHAPTER OF THE CYBORG LIZARD GUARDIANS

Killy barks, and her barks vanish into the vacuum of nothing. Bouncing off no walls. The Jingo Monitor lizards bark in response, then explode out from the wall. Blood gushes from the crack and lizards tumble over the ledge, sliding down the blood-slippery wall with nothing to grip on to. Some slink out and push us along the wall, or crawl on sucker-feet surrounding us. Their lights command us.

Behind the wall, the cyborg lizard guardians approach, demolishing the crawlspace. This is the sound they make:

Doosh.

Doosh.

Doosh.

They are demolition machines with big mechanical gnashing jaws and steel fists and armoured tails.

You left too soon, Dil. You saw this happening but you left us too soon. And now there is cold air and fresh wind that accompanies our doom. We will surely perish at the bottom. I will not meet Sunburst again. You will return to a Daff-less city. No Cyberia waiting for you either. And that's only if you come back at all.

These are the thoughts that run through my head, you inconsiderate fuck. If you were here I would throw you off this ledge again. You left too soon, and now the cyborg lizard guardians have come to punish us.

CHAPTER
INTRODUCING THE
JANKEN BROTHERS

There are three of them. Three cyborg lizard guardians. Three Janken Brothers. There is one out here on the ledge with us. The other two are mysteriously absent, yet it feels like they are here, like ghosts.

Janken Brother Number One: The Rock.
   Face like granite. Teeth big as my fists. Glass eyes through which the other brothers watch with hunger. He is King Cyborg Lizard. Tail like a wrecking ball. Titanium scales. Pylon legs cling to the ledge, the mass-density of his feet have a gravity of their own. The Orphanarium is his magnet. Hammerfists swinging. God of destruction.

Janken Brother Number Two: The Paper.
   Deafmute god of suffocation. Albino cyborg lizard. Wet pink eyes, blood and vitreous humour. No melanin. Electrolytes pump through him. The silent killer in the night. The shadow. The Watcher. The Waiter. He could have been right there on the wall and we wouldn't have known it. He watches the oxygen that leaves our lips. He waits for the right moment to steal it.

Janken Brother Number Three: The Scissors.
   Samurai lizard. Arch-angel of the knifeworld. Codename: Blade. Slick and smooth and sharp and fatal. Fierce as a dragon. Arms like katana. The swift guillotine machine. He is the colour of fire, constantly changing as a crystal changes colour. Skin

shimmering with reflections and refractions and capturing every body in his skin. Everyone shattered and cleaved in two and erased from the Orphanarium. His eyes are yellow, his tongue is long and red and forked. He smells of copper.

MURDER CHAPTER ONE

You're bleeding.

Janken Brother Number One is dead. The Rock is dead with your fingers wrapped around his neck and your blood dripping on his face.

You were not gone half an hour and you have returned a warrior.

"Time passes differently out there," you say. You sit on the ledge beside the dead Janken brother, dripping face-pulp down into the abyss. You push The Rock over the edge and he falls much faster than he should, like something is pulling him down. "The Jingo don't know what war is," you say. "They aren't protecting us from shit. They won't know what to do when the Elementals come."

His hammerfists damn near killed us. Crushed us or threw us off balance or what. It was an electrical storm that sent you back to us. Riding on the static of a crackling yellow cloud spearheaded by a lightning bolt harpoon, with a worn out, torn and bloodied black-and-white striped uniform, you have come back a new orphan. You stabbed him in the arm and sent one big meat-fist plummeting down. From there it was a blur of fists and sparks, and Killy's panicked barks, and fountain sprays of blood. The Monitor lizards scattered or fell to their death or vanished.

"The Elementals," you say. "They get inside your brain. They do things no living creature should be able to do. We cannot defeat them."

"They're already here, aren't they?" Cyberia asks.

"Some of them, yes."

29

"The World Cactus," Cyberia says.
"It was an Elemental, yes. And Plant-Boy."
And
Sunburst.

"What should we do?" Cyberia asks.
"What *can* we do? Nothing. If they want to, they will destroy the Orphanarium. We're nothing to them."
"Stop," Cyberia says. "Look. Out there."

Something moves.

THE SEAHORSE CHAPTER

Cyberia smiles, and the glass window in her head lights up and she points to something out in the desert. Her light shines out onto it. It is a man with the head of a seahorse.

In an instant, he is gone. Disappeared into a nest of trees. And the sky forms a cloud in the shape of a seahorse head around a silver moon eye. His body rises out of the desert, all dead trees and red sand. His moonlight eye blinds us, and banishes us from the outside world.

Everything is back to the heavy, tinted air. To the walls and walls of steel and concrete. This megastructure we call the Orphanarium. It grinds us down, and grinds us down, and grinds us down. The Seahorse Elemental does not want us on the outside.

The Paper and the Scissors are nowhere to be seen. They are likely still in that destroyed crawlspace at the edge, wondering where our scent has gone. We have been teleported to a distant hidden region of the Orphanarium. We are in a big ring of a room, surrounded by other banished Monitor lizards. In the centre there is a pylon that glows and spins and hums. The Monitor lizards look as confused as you and me and Cyberia. Killy is mindless to such things. The light from the pylon throbs, and Cyberia's light matches it. My head throbs like it's trying to produce a light of its own, but it hurts my skull. I lose my feet and you lose yours, and the Monitor lizards around us are thrashing about as they lift slowly upwards. I think we are losing our sense of gravity. And it is only the programming in Cyberia and Killy that lets them keep their feet.

I have never seen anything like this pylon before. It surrounds us with its dystopic rings. We drift up and the ceiling catches us and pulls us in. It is shaped kind of like a mushroom, electric strings catching us and sending us into spirals. I can't grab on to anything. I can't control where I'm going. Closer to the pylon, the spinning appears much faster and louder. Golden rings rise up and run along the roof until they reach the outer edge and fall down. The fear running through my head at this moment is that if I touch the pylon I will die. On the floor, on what looks and feels like the ceiling from here, Cyberia and Killy have not moved. Her head pulsing, Cyberia is caught in the pylon's trance.

THE BANISHED CHAPTER

We don't see it or feel it like Cyberia does, but the pylon has locked on to Cyberia's mind. It's building. It's spinning faster. That thing communicates with her on other levels we can't comprehend. It does that while it threatens to pull us others apart. Our flesh is its enemy. How this thing (an Elemental?) got here in the first place is a mystery.

Cyberia's body is pulsing, twitching, meanwhile we're writhing and contorting, hovering closer by the moment to that fierce spinning pylon. She's trying to shut it down. Her mind flickers as she accesses her technomancer programs.

The pylon tries to overload her. They push and pull. We close our eyes and hope Cyberia has the strength and the willpower.

We brace ourselves for impact, but the pylon dies down like the eventual end of a carnival ride. And the roof slowly comes down. Cyberia wakes and we fall. Rain of lizards. Hands and knees, Cyberia is gasping for breath. You and I are trying to gather our legs. We're shaking, faces white like we've got no blood left, stomachs feeling like they've been drained and relocated to our throats. The room spins viciously. Lizards scurry wild in all directions, no longer vicious, only victimised, vulnerable and exposed in this room. Through cracks in the walls they disappear, leaving us in the dark with the malevolent pylon. Killy is huddled small on the floor, quivering, flickering static like she's split herself between here and other places.

"That thing," Cyberia says, tapping her head. "It was talking to me."

"It's another Elemental," you say.

"Yes. It wanted me to call it Cynthia."

"What did it want with you?"

"I don't know," Cyberia says. "It said some strange things. Said I was special. That I was different. That we could be friends."

"That thing," you point at the pylon, at Cynthia. "Wanted to be friends?"

"Apparently."

What I'm thinking is why are Elementals coming into the Orphanarium? Why now? What are they doing here? Why do they care about us? I put my hand up to my forehead. Burning. Sweating. Stale air hanging still and clinging to my skin.

"If I were to assume what this is," you say. "It's that some of the Elementals, the smaller, weaker ones, are running off and having some fun with us. These are just the children. The mothers and fathers, the Major Elementals are outside, living on a completely different scale of life to us."

SUNBURST
CHAPTER TWO

Light floods through the cracks in the pylon room, blinding us. A white-intense fire. Kaleidoscopes of Sunburst flicker about violently before materializing in front of the killer pylon, Cynthia. She is here to save us from it. Her arms are solid sun-blades that stab and slice into the concrete and circuitry. She buries her arms up to her shoulders, and Cynthia flares up again, fast and red and violent. You and I float off again, and Cyberia, frozen in place and throbbing, clutches on to the fearful Killy, resumes her dialogue with her dying friend. Cynthia is stripped to shreds by Sunburst's light. Her destiny is gone. Sunburst reaches into her core, and Cyberia's window flickers with Cynthia as Cynthia is reduced to screaming circuitry, burning out in an epileptic fit.

This is Cynthia's attempt to overload Cyberia's programming and transfer herself into Cyberia's body. It is the technomancy that keeps her out. This is how, with Sunburst's help, we faced off an Elemental and won. And you and I fall to our hands and knees, Sunburst glowing in the centre of the room. Bright and full of life.

"Where did you come from?" she asks.

The voice appears in our heads, with no mouth to produce it. Just light.

"We were outside," Cyberia says. "And a seahorse god sent us here."

She nods. She is golden.

"You cannot be here," she says. "You must return to your homes."

"You were in the crawlspace," you say. "You were guiding

us earlier. Why?"

"You must ignore these misadventures. They were not meant for you."

"We have the Monitors after us. How are we supposed to ignore them?" you ask.

"Yes, that is unfortunate."

"And we don't even know where we are right now."

"I will show you the way back. The rest is up to you."

Sunburst tears a path out of the room and draws a trail of light down a hallway. At the end, a blank wall. She traces a line of light into the surface which marks an invisible doorway. It opens into the wide fields and gentle breeze of the farming sector. She walks with us, Killy bounding through the overgrown holographic grass and barking at the candylions as we climb the fence into their field, seemingly unaffected by the encounter with Cynthia.

Sunburst stops and says, "This is where we part ways."

She vanishes, and all the time she never once looked me in the eyes.

JANKEN BROTHER SHOWDOWN CHAPTER TWO

Deja vu. Candylions purr and stare. Deja vu all over again. Needle and skin. Spines and memories and sun-globes and far away wars. Deja vu. Deja vu. Deja vu.

Go Home was our instruction. We don't go. We don't get there. You don't think the war is for you anymore, and I don't think so either. We are caught up in our own war now. Cyberia's light flickers and her nostrils flare. Her features flush white and for a moment she looks like the shell of a robot. Red floods to her eyes and lips and swims through her fibre-optic hair. She looks like a fuse, dangerously awaiting friction.

"Someone's coming," she says.

Watching. Waiting. He curls around the fence, Janken Brother Number Two: The Paper. He is a stealth assassin. Full of surprises, tries to steal our breath away. He is swift and precise, before we see him there he whips thin vines at us. Just as the World Cactus has died/is dying/will die, we can not escape our fate. We are prisoners to our memories. Events beyond our control. Inevitability that hangs on a string, pulling at us. The vines constrict us. We fight but they only grow tighter. Here is something he prepared earlier – an assault on our minds. This moment is a blind spot in our memories. A haze of white noise we can't quite explain. He knows our future is short, not distant. He knows it is ugly and that we must embrace it.

There is a vine crushing my chest, and a vine around Cyberia's head, squeezing against her monitor, and there is also one around your neck, veins popping in your head, your eye ripe and ready to pop. There is a lot of blood in a small amount of time. Before I can tear myself free there is something else curling and squeezing around me. Janken Brother Number Two: The Paper, his tail snakes along like it has a mind of its own. Chop it off and you've got a headless snake. Chop it off. It is suffocating me.

My eyesight is popping and turning starry black and there is a crackling sound that is my bones. A tighter feeling I've never known. I'm waiting for a dream-state that never comes.

MURDER CHAPTER TWO

Janken Brother Number Two is dead. The Paper is dead with a knife in his chest, torso ripped to shreds. And you have killed two times, killed the Janken Brothers two times.

My eyes were popping black stars as Janken Brother Number Two became Boa Constrictor, a master of the art of suffocation. In the cloud-cluster of stars there was a single image peeping through. A bright red cupcake, soggy and dripping. Your mangled eye socket in my field of vision. Your bursted eyeball oozing out. Your other eye was locked on its target. Blur and hack and slash releasing the constrictor. Meaty ribbons on the ground. I don't know how many bones broke inside me. Tumbling tower falling down. Even you, my brother, can't keep me from falling down. In my body are bone splinters and in my head are the words: We All Fall Down We All Fall Down We All Fall Down We All And you, brother, wield a blade like a scalpel and face the tail-less Janken Brother with his smothering limbs. What was once a shard of glass from Cyberia's cracked monitor is now a weapon in your hands. Cyberia's throat is in the Janken Brother's fist while Killy is crouched in the grass amongst the frightened candylions.

You slash and his reptile skin splits. Acid spills out and sizzles on the ground. He leaps back, squeezes Cyberia tighter. Her window shatters and cycles through light and disconnected images like a popcorn machine. Random shards project chaos outwards, as if designed to induce seizures in her attackers. Fortunately her circuitry is bendable. Fortunately her tolerance for pain is high. With her neck in his fist she is a ragdoll. Her memory is ready to return to the mainframe. If her body is destroyed her memory can be downloaded into a new body, but she will not be the same Cyberia. In this body, she has her technomancy, and she commands Killy to be brave, to leap from the candylions and wrap her jaws around the Janken Brother's arm.

He thrusts his head back, a silent howl into the air.

He lets Cyberia go and leaves himself open for your backslash that peels his face open and the stab to the chest that finishes him off.

CROSSROADS CHAPTER

Meet me at the crossroads outside TNX noon tomorrow.

We can't escape our prophecies. Cyberia pushes your red cupcake eye back in and welds a patch over it. After Cyberia injects nano-bots into my body to protect my bones we lift the corpse of Janken Brother Number Two. Skin split and sagging and leaking. Safe for now, no alarms ringing, we bring this dead guardian to the old dirt intersection where no orphans go. We are at the crossroads outside TNX with the body of a Janken that needs disappearing. We take this moment to collect ourselves. We lay Janken Brother Number Two out on the ground cold and unfold him until he becomes an unrecognizable flesh sheet. We fold his body into the form of an origami swan.

Killy barks and licks the swan. Cyberia sits and scratches Killy's ear, playing through her programmed hypotheticals to figure out where we should go.

Your plan is to stuff him in a vent in an outlying sector of the Orphanarium that no one will bother to check. But the blood of a Monitor is pungent and in the vents the fumes will go places. They are already out to get us without us waving blood-stained hands and severed lizard claws in the air. I know a place. I know the exact place it has to be.

There are two things that have no place in the Orphanarium: Elementals and outlaws. We don't belong in here, same as how we don't belong out there. We have killed/are killing/will kill the lizards. We do the same to any other orphan here who tries to tear us apart. We let our dog chew on the origami wings. We use cactus spines to make our decisions for us.

Does that make us murderers?

You shake your head, no. We're survivors.
     Survivors of the vile machines that tried to capture us.
     Survivors of the megastructure that has consumed us
     (and continues to consume us).
     Survivors of the Janken Brothers three.

I have decided what I'm doing with the body. You can help me
or you can do your own thing. Same goes for Cyberia. Killy
has a mind of her own that exists outside these problems and
puzzles. She will most likely follow the smell of the swan. I will
bring it to the night sector where it will sleep forever.

THE DAMAGED
CHAPTER

You don't want to come with us. Your eye is throbbing and you're covered in gore. You want to go to the android markets, get a tune up while you're there. Try to blend in with the androids and orphans.

Cyberia, she says "yeah." The damage to her head is not pleasant. It leaks down her face and she pretends like it's nothing, but it's not nothing. She's pretty banged up and she should get some repairs done too. She says, "I'll come too, Dil."

Leaving me and Killy to dispose of the swan. I will meet you and Cyberia at the android markets later, maybe get my bones looked at.

We used to be just brothers. Cyberia was just a friend. Now, we are tied together through the Monitors that hunt us. We are tied by the Jingo. A mutual need to keep our distance from them. And people in the other parts of the Orphanarium carry on living their day to day lives. The Jingo are our protectors like jailers protect the incarcerated. They are our eternal controllers. This is the institution we were born into and have lived in like nothing mattered, until the World Cactus summoned us, and the Sunburst trail led us outside, and Janken Brother Number One fell out of his world.

I close my eyes and the image of him falling is right there. His body-mass gravity pulled him down fast, but he falls in slow motion in my memory. I gradually open my eyes. You and Cyberia are walking off to the android markets in slow motion. The swan at my feet, Killy licks it.

You turn back slowly and say, "Take care." A goodbye that stretches out forever.

ORIGAMI SWAN
CHAPTER
(OR NIGHT SECTOR CHAPTER TWO)

I wind up the swan and its flesh-paper wings flutter. It takes off down the path towards the night sector. Killy barks and jumps at it, trying to catch it in her steel jaws. The path bisects districts AKO and TNX. On one side, fields of crop and livestock flood with warm sunlight and honey tinting in the air. On the other, the cool blue-grey of steel and concrete, economical suns shining on factories and giant machines, slick oil fumes lifting into fans far above, creating cones of vapour that look like transparent pine trees. Ahead there is a black wall stretching all the way from the far edge of AKO to the far edge of TNX. Wall to wall, floor to ceiling, separating the night sector from the rest of the Orphanarium. And it is smooth and black like a mirror.

As we approach, an identical, yet darkened version of ourselves approaches from the other side. The flesh-paper-glass swan, shimmering Killy, and the glassified I come to meet us at the entrance. Going through is a matter of walking through the seamless revolving panels. We roll on through into the night sector and our mirror-selves disappear.

There is a hyper-saturation of tinting in the air. Violet. The night sector in MLO with the sprawling towers twisting into spires like giant conical shells. Conveyor belts pass from tower to tower, thousands of silver tokens on the silent belts, sleeping. The floor is a black silicon grid and it absorbs my footsteps and Killy's and it feels like we are ghosts in this place. This side of the Orphanarium is where people go for rest, for recharging, for retirement. There is a whole other city on this side for the night walkers, for the people that come here and don't want to go back. For us day dwellers, we have no need for the night sector while we are so young. The soft glowing night-lights track along the roof, casting their dim lights on this land. Everyone who is asleep right now is transformed and compressed into little silver coins, sleep tokens, and they come out the other side re-orphaned and refreshed. On the other side of the sleep towers is the distant blue and green glow of the Nightopolis, the city in the dark.

Janken Brother Number Two turns into a token and I toss him in with all the other sleepers and let the sleeping corpse rest in the token of an origami swan.

SUNBURST
CHAPTER THREE

The dim moon lights cast monolithic shadows of the towers on the ground that can't be seen but feel just as dark and heavy as though they could. One of these shadows rolls over me and my bones rattle as it tries to transform me into a token and put me to sleep.

I'm not going to sleep here. The coins in the towers and on the conveyor belts are restless. The air is quivering and the coins are shivering like something big is coming, feels like an earthquake. They're shivering and the sound of coin rattling on coin is muted, absorbed into the night sector air.

From the air comes a low, wailing siren, a loud 'wub-wub-wub-wub' noise, and the Jingo Monitor lizards are in here firing their light beams about wildly at the tokens that have been awakened back to their material selves. And the light beams trap all of us from going anywhere. Hung in their bright lights, we hear whispered rumours that an Elemental has entered the Orphanarium. But Jingo don't play with rumours. And they don't want us running around panicking or trying to hunt the creature down. And I know right here and right now that they aren't hunting Elementals. They're hunting us. Hunting me. I hold Killy quietly and stand still while they search the area for a gang of fugitives, a gang of three. I stand and wait and try my hardest not to look like one of us. My bones rattle gently and the Monitors march around us slowly. And then they turn the alarm off and lighten the tinting in the night sector. They slink back into the shadows with a lick of their lizard tongues and a shift of their lizard tails. In the instant the last Monitor turns its light off, there is the frame of a young girl carved out of light.

My Sunburst.

The people who were woken return to their sleep state, the origami swan settled amongst them. And my Sunburst explodes into the night sector like a gust of air, and blazes a trail of light to the city, calling me to join her in the Nightopolis.

RETURN OF THE PLANT-BOY CHAPTER

My bones rattle as I chase the light. I run. The running motion pulls my limbs apart. It pulls my bones apart. It breaks the nano-bots to dust. But everything will be fine once I reach the Nightopolis. Everything will be okay once I find my Sunburst. When the spit on my tongue evaporates from the heat blistering from her face, That is when I will be the closest I have ever been to the sun. I am driven by her image. I am compelled by her proximity.

The Nightopolis is alive with neon lights and insomniacs. Steam bellows from vents in the streets, signs in dozens of languages hang down across the street or plaster themselves on food carts pushing aromas from all over the Orphanarium. Some carts boast delicacies stolen from outside the wall. Men in trench coats sip luminescent drinks while chameleon vendors fry up their candylion burgers for the orphans and circuit board kebabs for the androids. You wouldn't believe this place if you saw it for yourself. But these people ignore the light passing by them like it's nothing, and they ignore me as I chase it into a building with a purple sign that flashes: THE BURNING CACTUS, with the image of a cactus wearing a sombrero that catches fire then flickers and dies and pops up again.

In the building, Sunburst is here with Plant-Boy, and they stare at me.

"You followed me?" Sunburst asks.

I nod.

"Are the Janken Brothers still after you?"

I nod.

"Two of them are already dead," Plant-Boy says. His burning roses look dull and lifeless in Sunburst's presence.

"The twin and the technomancer? That is a shame..." Sunburst blinks, and for a moment everything goes dark.

"No, not the orphans," Plant-Boy says. "The Jankens. Rock and Paper are gone."

"Where are your friends, boy?" Sunburst asks.

"They're in the android markets," Plant-Boy says. "They're safe, for now."

I want to tell Sunburst how I feel about her.

"Why do I bother talking to people while you're around?" Sunburst asks Plant-Boy. "I could just get you to write everything down and we could give up on dialogue entirely. What do you think of that?"

"You like the act of being social," Plant-Boy says.

"What do you think of that, boy?" she says to me.

I shrug. Her voice crackles and burns. It rides solar waves around the room.

"We should have left three minutes ago," Plant-Boy says. "Our boy here is going to have a bit of trouble getting back to his friends now." He says to me, "Head down, eyes up, you'll be ok. And if you see an egg rolling down the street, make sure you run the other way."

THE FIRE PENGUIN/ VAMPIRE PENGUIN APOCALYPSE CHAPTER

Chaos has descended upon the Nightopolis in full force. Food carts are strewn about the street, banners are torn and tattered and burning. A man in a trench coat finishes his drink before disappearing down an alley. The BURNING CACTUS sign is broken at my feet, and the image of the eternal cactus flickers as if dying, but it never does. In the streets there are fire penguins and vampire penguins absorbed in a turf war. The Monitors try to break them up but they can't do shit. The fire penguins conduct flames from their flippers and ceramic beaks. The vampire penguins perch on the rooftops like gargoyles with velvet wings and hurl neon letters down on their opponents.

Head down, eyes up. My bones are fragile. Killy knows this is not the place for her, and she pops out of here. She will find you in the markets, and once I get out of here, so will I. But half the street is blocked off with fire, and the other half with neon letters.

Head down, eyes up, I wander out through the flame-and-fangs skirmish, and I pass down the only clear street. And here, there are more brawling penguins, upturned carts and sunken letters. I follow the safest passages trying to block out the chaos around me, but it doesn't help when streets are getting blocked off everywhere, or when a burning flipper brushes against my side, or a vampire penguin flies too close to my head. I don't know if these creatures are Elementals or if they are just like us. I don't wait long enough to find out. I come to a street that ends in an alley. At the entrance to the alley is a man in a trench coat. He rolls an egg across the ground in my direction. I turn and run.

Five steps later, an explosion.

Head down, eyes up, running. Through the fire I run. The letters are hurdles and I leap through an 'O'. Sweat on my brow, smoke in my lungs, bones rattle with every pounding step. I'm running out of time and space. I'm running out of time and space. I'm running out of time and space. I'm running. I'm running. Before the penguins know I'm gone, I hit the mirror-wall.

CHAPTER SET IN THE ANDROID MARKETS

I am about to collapse by the time I reach the android markets. My bones don't want to hold me up any more. I drag my shattered frame into the bone palace where they agree to replace my bones with plutonium. They inject a solvent into my bones and drain them out, then melt the plutonium and inject it into the hollow cavities where my bones used to be. There are two hundred and six needles on the injection machine. One for each bone in the body. I climb into the harness and wait for the anaesthetic.

It doesn't come.

Two hundred and six needles enter my bones. Two hundred and six bones disappear. Two hundred and six plutonium bones replace them. They slide me into the freezer for my bones to harden.

When I come out, they attach a battery pack to the back of my skull. It energises my muscles into lifting and moving my heavy bones. When I walk out onto the street, you and Cyberia and Killy are waiting for me. Your temporary eye patch has been replaced with a permanent one. Cyberia's broken monitor has been replaced and the colour has returned to her features.

We rest in the market-sprawl beside a vendor selling electrolytic fish tanks and silicone jellyfish. The sun-globe tracks its way across the roof. You and me, and Cyberia and Killy. And a voice crackles through speakers throughout the market sprawl: Jan Ken Pon.

It crackles and swims and crawls inside my head like a centipede.

Jan Ken Pon.

It rips apart my skull and burns like a sentimental volcano. The image of Janken Brother Number Three bursts out of the window in Cyberia's head, a holographic manifestation of the physical Janken Brother floating in the space between us. And he says, "You killed my brothers, and now I will kill you. Jan Ken Pon." His hologram explodes in lights
    and bits of burning metal that feels real on the flesh, but is no more real than the sun in the sky outside.

THE HOLOGRAM CHAPTER AND FIRST DEATH OF CYBERIA

What we know we can attribute to a keen sense of future intuition developed through our interactions with the World Cactus and Plant-Boy. What we know is that Janken Brother Number Three: The Scissors is tracking us. We can not escape him forever. We will only die trying.

In this moment, sitting, stunned, confronted by the last remaining Janken, I am shaken out of time and into a place I can only describe as inevitability. A sensory overload. Slick ground, machine oils evaporating and drifting upward. Giant engines in constant motion. I don't tell you or Cyberia that I'm leading you into a battleground, nor do I tell you what results await us. We leave the android markets to the orphans. We enter the world of massive machines. Construction and destruction, world of endless repetition. When we arrive, Cyberia knows where this is from. She looks at me and knows this is the memory of hers I have seen.

Janken Brother Number Three finds us in the industrial district of TNX with the big ships moving slowly overhead on giant cables slowly moving overhead, casting big shadows on the ground like giant tombstones.

Here, the air is tinted red, and Janken Brother Number Three is not yet dead. The Scissors stands almost as tall as all of us combined. He is here, with eyes like black dragons and a face-plate like a waterfall. And he stabs Cyberia in the chest with his hands, and he tears her ribs inside out and she looks like a broken matchstick birdcage. She is crying, and her chest is filling with a rosy-coloured liquid, and the window in her head flickers a spastic orchestra of light. Her hands grab his, still grabbing her ribcage. The rosy-coloured liquid leaking down his arms and burning through his synthetic flesh.

MURDER: THE LAST CHAPTER

Cyberia's acid spills to the floor. It is warm and glowing and running from her chest down the Janken's arm and her whole body shakes with the fleeting energy of a mortally wounded android.

The Janken Brother says, "Where is your technomancy now?"

His blades are spinning in a wide, grotesque arc, arms still deep in Cyberia's leaking chest.

He says, "Where is your android magic for when the Elementals come?"

His blades split open Cyberia's face, amputate your arm at the shoulder and bisect it at the elbow, and slits my chest open like a bloody flower.

He says, "Who will protect you when they come to collect their harvest?"

I punch him in the back of the knees. Once, twice, he comes crashing down, twisting and collapsing, contortionist Janken.

He says, "You have brought war to the Orphanarium."

Janken Brother Number Three is on the floor, blades splayed and bloody, with wings made of crystal knives.

He says, "None of the weapons you have will be good enough against them."

And the big ships move slowly overhead on giant cables slowly moving overhead, casting shadows over you and me and Cyberia and Killy, and the blood stained cyborg lizard guardian.

He says, "There is nothing you can do but wait for them to come and claim what is theirs."

He laughs and we all bleed, and the shadows of the big ships consume us as the Orphanarium has consumed/is consuming/ will consume us. How the outside world crushes in upon us. How it threatens to destroy us. How you lay on the oil-slick floor with your arm in pieces and Cyberia is losing her life. How Killy is crouched beside her, licking her elbow. How I liberate the lizard with the weight of my plutonium bones.

The last remaining Janken, dystopian angel, being crushed by my boots stomping on his crystal wings. As you wrap your one good arm around his neck, he tries to pull away. And Cyberia pulls his arms deeper into her guts. He tries to stab and cut and pull himself free, but his arms are melting. His throat is constricted, his face turning blue. And my boots, stomping, crush up and down his spine. His head. And Janken Brother Number Three is dead.

THE SUBLIME ORPHANARIUM CHAPTER AND CONFLICT RESOLUTION

We are in pieces.

We know nothing.

We are nothing.

We have died/are dying/will die.

Here is us. We are here in the Orphanarium. No one is allowed outside. Here, people are born out of the air or made like computers and put together. Daff is me and Dil is you and together we are twins pulled from the same vacuum of space. Cyberia was our friend android. Perhaps we can put her back together some day. Our pet is called Killy, a cyborg dog who was born out of the air like you and me, but has since been built up with robot parts so she can live longer.

This is the way things are. And the way things are right now is all about the situation with the Elementals. They are gods of chaos and destruction. Of love and time and gravity and space. Gods of wings and flames and beauty and manipulation. We try so hard to stay alive but the chaos spills through the walls onto us.

There is no control.

And the shadows of the big ships move on and forget we are here in the sublime world of

The Orphanarium.

OUTSIDE

THE HALF HOUR SPINE CHAPTER

Why is there no furniture in your home?
    Why is there no light?
    Why has the flooring been torn up and dumped outside?
    Why have the windows been painted black?

I open the windows and purple tinted air leaks its way inside.

    What are these paintings on the walls?
    What are the paintings of the brightly coloured shuttles?
    What are the paintings of these golden machines?
    Where is this city painted in your hall?
    Who are all the children?
    Why are they all smiling?
    Why are they all laughing?
    Where did the giant gash in the ceiling come from?
    Why did you call me here?
    Where are you, Dil?
    Where are you?

When Cyberia was put back together you were gone. Her technomancy didn't work quite the same since. We didn't know where your head was at. What you were doing, where you were going, we had nothing. Cyberia and I drifted apart. I've seen her maybe two or three times since we separated. She's doing okay. And Killy is doing okay, too. I wish I could say the same for you.

The only thing in here which is not a painting or a wall or

floor or ceiling is a drawer. The only thing in the drawer is an envelope with "For Daff" written on it. A cactus spine rolls out into my palm. The twin spine to the one in my pocket. Dried blood and memories. Your memories. Hair is tied around the blunt end of the spine. It looks like my hair, your hair, my brother. A paintbrush of your memories. Murals on the walls. The moment where you leave us for the war. I breathe in the dust that stirs and sink the spine into my wrist.

I miss you.

CHAPTER AT THE BOTTOM OF THE WALL

I'm sliding down. I'm sliding down. I'm sliding into your skin, down the wall. Looking up, there is myself and Cyberia shrinking away on the ledge, as gravity has its way with the body that I'm in. I haven't seen you for so long, and now I have become you. The fresh outside wind is a distant memory that floods back stronger and more vibrant than ever.

We slide down the wall, leaving the Orphanarium behind. A long way down there is red sand stretching out into desert. Dead trees scratch their white limbs to the sky by the thousands. The skeleton forest. As we slide closer to the ground it smells scorched, burned. The air is warmer even though there are no sun-globes tracking across the sky.

Breaking through the wind, Monitor lizards rain down past us and splatter on impact with the ground. Blood rains down with lizards and lizard parts, and they splatter an orchestra of noise below. The ground is hot, like something beneath the ground is heating it up and radiating it up through our feet. The heat rises and dries up all the moisture in the air. The smell of charcoal. The smell of cooked lizard. Of boiling blood. We take to walking along the wall, looking for something that's neither wall nor sand nor tree nor sky nor splattered corpse. What we're looking for, I don't know. In the wall, we glimpse ourselves, reflection on a sleek surface. This is the first time I have seen you in a long time. For a moment, I am convinced that the person in the reflection is not you. It is me. This is my memory. My future. My destiny. For a moment. This is the image of you suspended in the past. I am merely trapped in your body. We walk on, following the wall, brushing our fingertips along the surface.

And then this idea hits our brain: *We are* outside *the Orphanarium. We are exploring new territories never before witnessed by the general population inside it. We will follow the wall until it proves nothing more to us. Then we will wander out into the desert, the graveyard formed out of skeleton trees. If we find nothing else there, we will sift the earth for answers. We will try to find what it is that heats the surface. If we don't find answers, we will dig a hole large enough to bury us and we will sleep. When we wake we will continue exploring this world outside the walls. There is a war out here somewhere. We will find it and figure out what madness fuels it. We will not rest.*

These are the thoughts that run through your head. These are the thoughts that I read. Then our mental plans for expedition are suspended. We catch the image of a light further along the wall. It pulls us in. We run to it.

THE ORPHAN ARMY
CHAPTER

As we come closer to the light, we see that it is positioned at the centre of a large crowd. The heat in the ground seems to increase the closer we come. The light becomes harder to see through the density of the crowd, more streaked. As we get closer to the crowd we begin to notice certain inconsistencies. Static. Slight blurring. Occasional shakes and tremors. Flickering and zoning out. They are almost translucent. Silently facing the light as if expecting it to do something. The crowd consists of orphans like us—cyborgs, androids, lizards, people—all wearing black-and-white striped uniforms. Standing still.

We enter the mass, brushing our way through the crowd. Where there should be touch is an electrical hum with no resistance. The crowd is populated entirely by holograms, yet we can't quite make out the source of the light.

We pass our hand through the ghostly shoulder of one hologram and ask, "What's this all about?"

They reply with a stern, "Shh."

We move further through the holographic crowd and closer to the light. The heat keeps rising, and the light seeping through the crowd grows brighter.

This must be the Orphan Army, you think.

I would call that a fair assessment.

That light...

We're getting close to the front of the crowd. The light shines bright, white hot radiation through the crowd.

That light...

We sweep through the tangled bodies of the holographic mass—arms and legs and tails crowded and overlapping and passing right through each other. Hot and sweaty passing through the phantom bodies of the crowd, the light forms solid shapes, limbs of its own.

Sunburst?

It isn't her. This light-creature is big and old and slow. Sunburst is swift and graceful and much more beautiful.

We push our way through to the front of the crowd, a tight circle around this light. She is much bigger and hotter than we could have imagined. She is burning us. She is killing us with this heat, yet your body refuses to move. She stares at us and we feel our cheeks filling with hot air, our head becoming the ash from the fires of a thousand sun-globes. Our lungs draw in only burnt air, peeling and smouldering at our throat, the inside of our chest. She stares at us and blinds us.

And then...

Darkness.

A cool wind blows through the crowd. The ash and burning and blistering dissipates into cool. In the centre of the crowd there is a pile of ash where the light-creature used to be. Within the pile of ash, a faint glow. Up bursts a new light, a phoenix warrior. This is not Sunburst, but it is definitely of the same genetic material.

"Soldiers," the light warrior calls out.

Her light is much softer, yet she looks fiercer. Like the death and rebirth has made her more resolved, more defined.

"Your mission is simple. Do not return until you have defeated the Elementals." The crowd cheers.

Why do they cheer?

"It is now time for you to follow your brothers and sisters, go and join them in the battlefields." The crowd stomps and claps and cheers and bangs their chests.

Where are their weapons?

The holograms mutate into a polymorphic mass, passing

through itself, charging into the desert. The light warrior smiles and waves.

We walk up to her and you say, "The army always dies, yes?"

She nods her radiant head. "The army always dies."

"Why?"

"It is the way of the world. Look at the Orphanarium."

The Orphanarium wall is crumbling, infected, sick. Elementals hang off it, breaking chunks and raining them down or destroying barriers with just their light-beam fingers or their chaos frequency voice boxes.

"Go and fight a beautiful war, and have yourself a beautiful death." She touches our chest, filling it with warmth, and turns us towards the army marching away from the wall. She bows her head and transforms into a small star whizzing up into nothing.

Here we go exploring the great beyond.

THE BULLETPROOF CHILD CHAPTER ONE

With the warmth of the light warrior inside us, we run into the bone orchard. Dead trees drawing sharp-shadowed images in the sand. The hologram people marching ahead of us seem less like an army and more like a suicide cult. We are unsure if these people are the past, the faded ones, the dead ones of us, or if they are the future suicide soldiers, or a combination of both. But perhaps they are just like you. This war is a compulsion. A black hole sucking us in. If nothing else it serves to fulfil your prophecies. But you must have known you weren't going to die, right?

Right?

Your phantom army brothers and sisters march through the orchard. We run to catch up. There is one child with slick black skin who is not like the others. Not a phantom. Not a hologram. Not a ghost or a spectre. Slick black skin, his uniform seems to grow out of it. Our reflection in the side of his head.

"I have never seen anyone like you before," you say.

He glances at us. "There's a lot of people like that around here."

"Everyone else is a hologram."

"Like I said, there's a lot of people like that around here. They just aren't here *right now*. You're not in your uniform."

"I don't have a uniform," you say. "I didn't join the army. I'm just sort of... here."

"Why?"

"I don't know."

"My name is the Bulletproof Child," he says. "Who are

you?"

"I'm Dil," you say. We shake his hand. It feels hard like glass, but not brittle.

We move through the bone orchard, the trees like orphan figures, skeletons clawing at us and trying to draw us in and trap us and draw us under. We follow their shadows through the orchard, with the shadows of phantom fruits hanging on the ground like a time frozen in prosperity.

"Want to know a secret?" he says. "Nothing can penetrate my skin. The commander pulled me aside before the war and told me that if anyone were to survive this war it would be me. Because of my skin."

"That sure is something," you say. "Where did the Orphan Army find you?"

The Bulletproof Child shrugs and says, "We just sort of came here and signed up. Nothing special."

"Just something you had to do."

"Yeah, that sounds about right."

"And you're the only Bulletproof Soldier?"

"Yes. I can protect you, if you'd like. At least until you find a weapon to defend yourself with."

"Or until I die."

"Yes, or until you die."

Whatever comes first.

Ahead, a large holographic lizard soldier brushes past a branch, and the phantom fruit falls and becomes visible, solid. A peach tumbled at the feet of the soldier. The trees rattle as he picks it up. The sand at his feet is shifting. He sinks to his waist, struggling.

"Help me up," he calls to his friends, his voice a polyphonic wail, warped over time. They walk away. We watch for a moment, watch the phantom sinking. The tree absorbs him and takes his being into its image. Lizard limb branches.

Helmet dangling. Lizard tails and skulls etched into its bones. The trees surrounding us take on a more sinister image. We keep walking. The war has claimed its first victim.

CHAPTER WHERE YOU RIDE A TRAIN

On the other side of the bone orchard, we have lost a whole collection of hologram soldiers. Most were caught by trees and trapped by phantom fruits, the phantom harvests pulling them down while the rest of us kept moving. Whether we wanted to help or not, we couldn't. Their deaths belonged to a different time. Some soldiers just disappeared. Vanished. Like, you see them, then you turn away, then you look back and they're gone. Like their hologram disintegrated in an instant.

We stick with the Bulletproof Child through the orchard, beyond which is an old, decaying train station, a ghostly train at the platform billowing toxic smoke into the sky. Alone on the station, just the two of us (you/me, and the Bulletproof Child), standing on the platform. The doors open like lungs releasing stale air, flesh walls with hanging tendons, the entrance is an industrial meat grinder slick with blood and gore and chrome mechanisms. Entering the train means instant death.

I don't want to get on the train. I do not want to get on the train. I do not want. I do not want. I do not want.

We wait back.

I do not want to be crushed to death.

"Aren't you coming?" the Bulletproof Child asks.

We gulp. Our stomach is tightly knotted, squeezed. Sweat spilling from every pore. We shake our head. "There's no way."

"Come on," he says. "It will be okay. I've done this dozens of times before."

There is no way. There is no way. There is no way. There is no fucking way. What if the train is sending us to slaughter? The grinder will kill us instantly. No way out. Where is it going anyway?

Does it matter? Do I even want to know anyway? Probably not. What other options do I have? Death in the orchard heading home. Death on the platform waiting for another train. A sudden death boarding the war train. Okay. Okay. Okay. Okay. Okay. Okay. Okay. I'm coming.

On the platform, the train. The carriages packed with holographic soldiers. I thought you were more confident than this. We can not turn back now. We are driven by inevitability. We can wait on the platform alone, wait for something to happen. Or we can get on the train with the holographic soldiers.

We've done it all before. Plucking up the courage to make that first step again.

The Bulletproof Child pushes us onto the train, a hard shove in the back. The guy who promised to protect us. The grinder pulls us in to its crushing chute. The gears grab us and tear our flesh, gets the skin winding its way through the grinder. Bones popping apart as our arm parts and leg parts become swallowed and mangled. Until our torso becomes mince meat and splintered spine and ribs. Burst organs, crushed and shredded windpipe. No breath, our jaw is dislocated. Our eyes pop bright with stars. Hot sizzling flesh and blood. We smell the wet. We see the pit on the other side, the lumps of minced bodies over there, and we are rebirthed on the other side unharmed as a passenger on this train.

There is so much space here. The walls are reinforced and armoured. A concealed shell inside the fragile skeleton of a small passenger train. Phantom people are sitting on benches on the floor, on the walls and ceiling, hanging in the air. There are no windows. The lights are dim.

A large man with a black sphere face walks down the aisle approaching us. He pauses, staring at us. He jabs his finger up, indicating us to stand. He pulls a gun from his jacket and shoots us. The bullet hits us in the chest but it doesn't hurt. It bursts into a web of light and wraps around our body, covering us in a black-and-white striped ballistic uniform matching all the others. He punches a ticket for us, for the Bulletproof Child, and moves on. At the end of the compartment, he disappears into the meat grinder in the wall.

The war train rumbles into operation.

THE DINING CHAPTER
AND MR. MOON

The Bulletproof Child stands up and indicates that we follow him. Passing the passengers in our carriage (some real, some holographic): a man with a lion head, a crab-shelled person with pincer hands, a woman with jellyfish hair, a row of silent technomancers.

"How many soldiers are there?" you ask the Bulletproof Child.

The jellyfish woman grabs us by the collar and drags our face close to hers. Salt-water brine stench on her slimy skin. "We're not soldiers, my dear friend, we're prisoners. *Prisoners!* We're sacrifices to the Elemental Gods. Play along for now, but always be on the lookout for an exit."

Her voice stings our ears, our head. Our skin.

"Fuck!" you yell, swatting a tendril of her hair off our cheek.

The jellyfish woman cackles and leans back.

A hand grabs ours and pulls us away. "Sorry," the Bulletproof Child says. "I thought you were following right behind me. Some of the people they've recruited..."

"They're mad," you say.

"Yes," a smooth black grin folds onto his face. "They're *mad.* They're not all *Mr. Moon* mad though."

We enter the dining carriage, where a variety of roast meats, spices, and sweet breads assault us with their combined odours. The carriage is filled with gluttons, binging on the buffet, flailing hands and greasy fingers. Above the buffet table is a wet neon sign boasting "the finest foods in the Orphanarium," dripping glowing flavours into sizzling pots of self-replenishing dishes.

"Grab a plate," the Bulletproof Child says.

We load up on lizard stew, pineapple pudding, and cyborg meat (authentic silicon, no substitutes). A glass of candylion milk. Strips of decadent night-mole jerky. We carry it over to the table Bulletproof Child is sharing with a strange old creature.

"Mr. Moon," he says, "This is Dil."

The man has a crescent-shaped head, cratered and dusty, formed out of grey space rock.

"Dil, huh." Mr. Moon sounds like he's been gargling concrete for forty years. "I knew a Dil once. Piece of shit, he was."

"Who is this guy?" you say.

"Irrelevant. I'm a guy on a train. You get three questions. No time to waste when there's good eating food waiting for us."

"You're some sort of oracle, right?" you say.

"Is that a question?"

We shake our head. "No, whether you're an oracle or not doesn't matter. I know this all in dreaming. The World Cactus. That was *my* oracle."

"Yeah, what's your point? Three questions, go."

"Everything I do feels like it's predestined. I am compelled to act out the dream. Does the dream differ in any way from reality?"

"How has it played out for you so far?"

We shrug. "About the same. I suppose. That would mean anything you tell me now I already know from the dream."

"That is a plausible theory."

"Where is the train heading?"

"Where do you think it is heading?"

This carriage has windows. Large ones swallowing most of the wall. We seem to be inside some sort of city. An all-consuming rock-ceiling above our heads. Flickers of passing pylons performing an epileptic dance with the violent giant dwarf sun-globes scorching the landscape to bleach-white and ruin crumble pies, melted fudge steel warped and puddled beneath the windowed floors. Behind us, a blank wall. In front, a blank wall. We speed into it, into a long dark tunnel where the only light is the 'finest foods in the Orphanarium' sign and the neon sauces in our foods, stained on our uniforms throughout the carriage, lighting up our stomachs, the act of being in the carriage transforms our flesh into windows. At the end of the tunnel, a sky bridge. A giant's mouth hanging from a cliff, decapitated. Deep below us is forest floor, scorched with violent flames from the devils who are trying to murder us before we can murder them. The bridge is gone and we are rolling on a battlefield plain. Blood lubricates the tracks. Elementals forming cyclones ripping through black-and-white striped giant orphan warriors. Technomancers floating and cutting through Elemental flesh with their laser minds. Occasional buildings floating and landing and moving and growing all around us. Mr. Moon waiting for his answer.

"Castle Nothing," you say.

Mr. Moon bows his head. "You have one more question."

"I have no more questions for you, old man," you say.

"Very well. May your meal be both nutritious and delicious."

"I have a question for the Bulletproof Child."

Mr. Moon pauses for a beat, allows a smile to creep across his crater-mouth. "Proceed."

"Bulletproof Child, tell me about your time at war."

"That wasn't a question," he says.

"That wasn't an answer. You've had to fight in this war before, haven't you?"

"Yes. More than a dozen times. Since I survived my first war and brought back a failed mission, they sent me out with the next group. And the next, again and again. Each return another failure. Each return a lone survivor. I've taken to using my skill set to protect my fellow soldiers, but I have had no luck as of yet."

"Are you an Elemental?" you ask.

Mr. Moon places his moon-rock hands on the table and says, "That is enough questions. Hands on the table, palms up."

We put our hands on the table and receive a tiny cloud of mist.

CHAPTER OF THE SEAHORSE MAN AT THE END OF THE LINE

The train rumbles to a standstill. Lights glow bright white. The white bursting spectrum of light consumes everything and spits us out on a train platform at the end of the line.

The train platform is empty but for us, the Bulletproof Child, and a stranger in a beige trench coat, sitting on an olive coloured bench. His head is covered in bony grooves. Sunken eye sockets. Bulbous eyes emerging. Leathery/leafy hair protruding from the ridges.

The Bulletproof Child tells us that we each have our own missions. The train has dropped us off exactly where we need to be.

The wind is cold, refreshing.

"My mission is to protect you," he says.

The man looks up at us.

I recognise him. I've seen this man before. The Seahorse Elemental, who banished us from outside the Orphanarium.

He nods slowly, as if understanding what I'm thinking, what you recognise through memory. His body warps and winds rapidly across the platform and he stands in front of us, extending a hand.

We shake it. Cold, clammy, like the sick old orphans of the Night Sector. His presence is illuminating. The silver moons of his eyes. Unblinking gaze.

Our hands still gripping, you say to the Bulletproof Child, "He is an Elemental, therefore he is our enemy. Right?"

We pull the mist cloud from our pocket and aim it at the

Seahorse Elemental, a warning. With his free hand, he rolls our fingers back around the cloud, keeping it safe.

"We choose our own enemies, Dil," the Seahorse Elemental says, "Or they choose us." He smiles and extends his free hand to the Bulletproof Child.

In this instant we are plunged into ice-cold ocean. We are banished once again. We are milked into a sea of liquid love. We are killed with the kindness of seafaring moons. We are beautifully splintered from this world and painstakingly rewritten into another, taking the ocean with us. Walls form from the ocean, sea-foam turns to ceiling and floor. Carpets, furniture. The ocean washes away, a receding wave into a hall of Nothing.

CHAPTER SET IN CASTLE NOTHING

Being banished isn't half as bad the second time around. In Castle Nothing, nothing is bad. Nothing is good.

"Do you feel that?"

"What?"

"Nothing."

"No."

"Me neither."

Echoes out to nothing. Paintings on the walls of nothing in particular. Wallpaper following no exact pattern. No texture to the strip of red carpet that runs down the hall. Staircase that spirals into nothing. Portrait of Sunburst, gazing out into nothing. The slight heat radiating from the portrait warping the canvas. Windows that open out to empty fields stretching to horizons that go nowhere. A solid gold brick embedded in the stone wall. A tiny sun in a giant room, about which miniature planets sweep around. We walk so close past it we can almost touch it. The sun burns just from looking at it. The planets fizz as they spin past, like they're dissolving in the atmosphere of the room. All of them gas giants. Or dwarfs. Castle Nothing Solar Systems.

More portraits of Sunburst. Some on her own. Some with a sun family. Brothers and sisters. Greater relatives. All of them burning stars. Mouths like cosmic bombs. Delta rays casting out the essence of oblivion. Portrait with a lover. Children of their own. Children of the billion-year calendars. All stars. All standing. All smiling. All gazing into nothing. Bright light warping canvases, smouldering hardwood frames, bleaching the canvas white, the wallpaper blossoming outward white. Golden eyes piercing gaze into nothing.

Laughter and charcoal. In a flash, a sun child bursts through a wall, black burn mark silhouette. Disappears into the opposite wall, silhouette and remnants of a dying flame. Plume of smoke. Another child bursts through in chase. A string of sun children following. One sun child comes to a standstill in the hall. "Why are you standing around for?" she says.

"Come join us," another one says.

They grab our hands and run through the opposite wall, burning themselves through the other side, burning us with them. Like passing through a curtain of molten lava.

THE SUNBURST FAMILY HISTORY CHAPTER

Girl on fire. Sunburst was born out of a dead star, her father who released his energy then became nothing. He died and birthed her into his galaxy. She is light in the darkest places. She is radiant. She is here with us in this room filled with sun people. An astronomical reunion. She turns to us and smiles. Lips golden and warm.

She says, "I'm so glad you could come."

It feels like a dream (of something unreal, not from a memory recalled from the World Cactus). It feels like underwater brush-strokes of perfection.

"I would love for you to meet my son, but I don't know where he is right now."

"I hope you find him soon," you say. "I'd love to meet him."

"Welcome to my family," she says. "Today is my millennium birthday, the day my father died birthing me a thousand years ago. His name was Sun-Dragon. He lives on inside me."

"You still look so young," you say.

Her cheeks swell red. Some of the children giggle. The rest are hiding under tables or flame dresses or bursting through walls at high velocity.

"You are too kind. I like who you are now, but you will change, sweet boy."

We smile. For a moment I forget she is talking to you. "I will *not* change," I say. "I love you, Sunburst. You are my eternal light."

No words come out. This is a dream-state which I have no control over. This brother-body which I am currently caged in. No one in the room hears my declaration, yet for a moment, I feel Sunburst's gaze turn from you to me. A soft amber twinkle in her eye like she knows someone else may be inhabiting your body. She looks away, and turns to the drinks table behind her. She has two orange drinks in tiny glass tumblers, and she passes one to us.

CHAPTER OF
THE FIRST CHILD

It burns our tongue, our mouth, our throat, through our body, burning. Our eyes, our lungs, our heart. Our cradle. Our temple. Our oesophagus. Our sarcophagus. Our home. Our moon. Our greater solar system. Our universe in the needle of an estranged brother burning. Darkness swells, forming spaces where you and I exist together with nothing else. Neither of us can form words to define this space.

A spark, a fire growing forming into the image of Sunburst. A volcano exploding. A horizon beyond which the mountain giants sleep. A sun eclipsing into a freshly populated world.

"Where did everyone go?" you say?

Burning ash breezing over our bodies, brushing our shoulders, arms, fingertips. Ash and smoke in our nostrils, tongue, lungs. Our army uniform is sticky with sweat. Sunburst's burning star-face burns close to our face, nose tickled with harsh flames, and she draws us into a charred-corpse inducing hug.

She whispers an inferno into our ear, "the Elemental Empire took my son from me." She hugs us tighter, our uniform smouldering and flaking, crackling, blistering, material leaf-dancing to the ground with flesh clinging to it. Molten tears roll down her cheeks. "The Elemental Empire kidnapped Sunchips and took him to the Sky Jaws."

"Where are the Sky Jaws?" you ask, "We can go together. We can go rescue him."

Sunburst points at the dark blue sky, penetrated by neon stars cutting through the void. In one chunk of sky there is a gaping hole where a giant star-mouth bares its dripping teeth. "I can't leave Castle Nothing or else the Empire would know. He'd be as good as dead before we could leave the ground. It has to be you, Dil."

"What do I do?" you say. "What *can* I do?"

Sunburst pulls a child from the air. "Take this child with you. He is Platinum. He will help you find Sunchips. He is a good child."

Platinum looks like a marionette made from glass tubes and polished chrome. His eyes are purple, and his brain computer sends bright signals throughout his fragile-looking body. He reminds us of Cyberia.

"What about the Bulletproof Child? Where is he?" you ask.

"He will find you when the time is right."

A loud, heavy cloud of smoke consumes everything around us, choking our lungs to rot, banishing us outside Castle Nothing. Smoke swirling to a clearing where Platinum leads us down a well-worn path.

"Where are we going?" you ask.

Platinum points at the mountain ahead of us.

"What about the Sky Jaws?"

He shrugs. "You'll see when we get there." His voice is tubular, like a robot through a concrete tunnel.

"And Sunchips?"

"Sunchips is not in the Sky Jaws."

THE ELEMENTAL EMPIRE CHAPTER

The Elemental world is split into quarters. Four children to own the legacy of the world. Four fathers to steal them away and to own the world for themselves.

ONE:

Platinum is the child of glass and electricity. Of technomancy and silicone and light. Child of the Orphanarium. It is of great concern that he seems unconcerned with the state of the Orphanarium or the outcome of the war. His father is the father of the creatures who tried to kill us for breaching the walls of the Orphanarium. Who will try to kill us. The Janken Brothers.

Platinum's father is the Janken Father. He is the father of all androids in the Orphanarium. The father of all cyborgs. His children, real children, are pulled from the warm tinted air, from the vacuum of space which creates us all. Janken Father is our father, a chrome cyborg dinosaur with technomancy powers to create or destroy cities in heartbeats. To wrap his giant monster palms in space and produce new life. To create barriers through which no other Elementals should be able to pass.

TWO:

Pacifica is the child of the ocean and all the things in it. She is the child of whales and sharks. The child of sunken ships. The child of kraken. She is the child of the great Sky Jaws, a world removed from our own—isolated like the Orphanarium—a great ocean empire in the sky. Her hydromancy powers are immeasurable.

Pacifica's father is the Skypool Giant. He is the father of the Sky Jaws empire. His children are the children of civil war and of refuge seekers. His empire is a vast ballistic battleground. His arms are wide as the sky forming oceans of fists to rain down on his enemies. His face is a great wild tsunami consuming everything.

THREE:

The third child is a hybrid child split in two. He has aged a mystery. Mr. Moon and the Seahorse Elemental are the uncanny twin child. Child of moon and earth and mountain. Rock like no other. A transformative space fish and an unchanging space rock. Elements of both overlapping and folding over each other. Both existing in no place in particular but the one they're in. Come together in youthful procession to form the Moon Child, the Moon Child's youthful procession brings life to his split identities.

Their father is the Moonhorse Juggernaut. He broke off parts of his crusty body to make his child. He split them in half and made one a moon man and one a seahorse child. He left his legacy shining in the sky. He came to earth and began crafting cities for no one in particular. He crafted doorways out of air and formed windows with his hands and planted them in the walls. With two thumbs and nimble fingers, he sculpted statues to look like all the things that brought him happiness. A sculpture of life. A sculpture of love. A sculpture of time. A sculpture of death. A ring of statues of all his friends standing so tall and proud and so close to his heart.

FOUR:

You know the fourth child, Sunchips. Fireworks spiralling, neon cartwheels into the night. You know the fear and love of his eternal mother, Sunburst. Her tears that melt the earth right through to its core. Burning pits around which the faithful gather. The long nights of waiting. Sunchips is a crimson spirit surfing the solar waves that resonate through this earth. He is growing and expanding, filling his potential as the fourth child of a dream foretold.

His father is his mother's father. A lump of burning gas spitting fireballs of children and his children's children. Dying and consuming sons and daughters, friends and enemies, consuming. Sun-Dragon, the apocalypse's nightmare, dawning horizons a billion times more beautiful than he. Creating vapours and ash and molten rock in his wake. Gnashing teeth of hot steel and scales made of molten glass. Shimmering in the light reflecting and refracting, producing, projecting. He will kill you.

Across millions of years they battle for control against an army which rises through the dust and the meadows, the deserts and destroyed cities, coming from the furthest reaches of space, the Android Wizards.

BULLET-BOY OF VANISHING MOUNTAIN CHAPTER

Platinum, and you, and I. We walk up the mountain on a path of moondust. Remnants of a distant past, a big chunk of the grey rock falling down and crumbling down, and crumbling down, and crumbling down until it is sand and the sand is used to sweep the path up the mountain. In the night, it is illuminating. He says this place is called 'Vanishing Mountain'. He doesn't say why, but he doesn't tell us to stop asking questions. About half way up, the questions begin answering themselves. The mountain below us seems more distant, more transparent than before. It might be the light around this time of night, yet the path still shines like a river of floating stars. The mountain is vanishing beneath our feet.

As we ascend, a fear of falling grows within us. The feeling that one wrong foot on the path, and we slip, we fall, we don't tumble down the mountain like a ragdoll. We plummet like a fucking boulder. We shatter into dust like a chunk of moon falling out of the sky. One wrong move and we vanish along with the mountain.

Platinum teaches us the meaning of the word 'Enlightenment'. He says we won't know what it means until we go into the Sky Jaws. Until we know true loss. Until we know how true loss brings growth, brings compassion, brings love. He touches our elbow. His fingertips feel cold, somewhat electric.

"Where did you come from?" you ask.

"You were there when you met me," he says.

"But are you one of us or one of them?"

He shrugs. "I am who I am. What is the difference?"

"Did you come from the Orphanarium?"

He nods. "One of us."

At the top of the mountain, a creature greets us. This is Bullet-Boy:

Chrome eyes on an otherwise featureless face. His body is a doppelganger for ours. His presence is transformative, explosive, aerodynamic. Gunpowder cologne overwhelming him. We shake his outstretched hand, don't squeeze too tight, for the fear he might combust. It feels like he can rip through anything. Except, maybe, a Bulletproof Child.

"This is my village," he says. "These are my people. Tonight we will fly into the Sky Jaws. You will come with us."

We nod.

We enter the village, following the jet-streams in the wake of Bullet-Boy's velocity. The village is chrome pillars on an obsidian plateau. Everywhere is a reflection of us, of you. Platinum's polished glass exoskeleton reflects the mountain village, reflecting him. Infinite hallways. Infinite Bullet-Boys. Infinite chrome pillars. Infinite plateaus. Infinite Platinums. You and me, we are infinitized over and over by the mountain village reflecting.

Up ahead, Bullet-Boy's vapours dissipate. He stops in the centre of the village and points above us into the Sky Jaws. A gaping hole waiting to swallow us up. To deliver us to new realities and destroy us in the most beautiful way possible. This is what it means to gaze into the void. We do not yet know what Enlightenment really is.

SKY JAWS CHAPTER

There is you and me, Platinum and Bullet-Boy, all sitting in the chrome village of the Vanishing Mountain, staring at the Sky Jaws. Bullet-Boy tells us he's been there many times. He used to live there as a child. You ask if he's been banished from there. Because we have been banished. We are being banished. We will be banished from the Orphanarium. For us, banishment is a way of life. But he has not been banished in the way that we know it. The chrome village of the Vanishing Mountain is a refugee village. He returns to the Sky Jaws every three cycles to see if his home is safe for his people yet. It was not safe the last time. Or the time before that. From the first time, it has not been safe. In fact, he thinks, things may be getting worse. Every three cycles the Sky Jaws ingests him. Every three cycles it spits him out.

This time, however, is not about refuge and return. This time, he'll take the entire village off this scorched earth—this shimmering chaosphere, this death of a planet by ritual suicide, exploding dragons—their makeshift homes on the vanishing mountain, and for better or worse, will fight for their right to return to the Sky Jaws.

The village people come out surrounding us, a nightmare collection of odd images and strange talents. These people all look somewhat like Bullet-Boy, with their doppelganger bodies which look just like ours. Their heads are fish heads, lion heads, torch heads, rain cloud heads, atomic cluster heads, bomb heads, crater heads, sun drowning heads, eclipse heads, and shuddering vision heads. Their hands make shapes like paper aeroplanes flying through silicon waterfalls. Their hearts carved with hope.

Some of the refugees are families. Young children. Women.

Elderly people. It is hard to tell with their doppelganger bodies, but their faces warp and distort, they wrinkle with age. Their bodies move with a bumbling lack of awareness, a skill that all newborns naturally possess. We gather on the obsidian plateau on the Vanishing Mountain, and a strangely organic industrial wind comes through, blowing through the pillar houses and in between the limbs of all of us gathered here. We all sway to the hollow industrial breeze music, a tribal refugee dance embracing our inevitable future as a war memorial.

CHAPTER OF THE NEON ROCKETS

We are all a children of dance. Vanishing Mountain is a ghost, a whisper. The shining plateau reflects the Sky Jaws, with the hundreds of doppelganger feet dancing over its cosmic maw. We chisel a new dance into our DNA. We climb mountains for fun and make peace with refugees. We sing with the industrial wind and our movements tell the refugees the story of how we existed in the Orphanarium and how we experienced the spiritual awakening/suicide/metamorphosis of the World Cactus and its memory spines. The refugees tell their story of letting go. They move their bodies, acting out their journey from the Sky Jaws. Their images reflected, being sucked down into the mountain. The Neon Rockets that brought them to this new world. The Neon Rockets around which they built a mountain with uncertain properties. They crushed the moon of their homeworld and swept a path up the mountain that would shine forever, that would serve as the mountain's spine.

Their dance says, "The Neon Rockets are inside the mountain, and they will return us to the Sky Jaws."

Their dance says, "The Neon Rockets are inside all of us. They are our link to home."

Their dance says, "They are our past, our present, and our future."

Their dance says, "We must go now."

Bullet-Boy propels himself into the surface of the obsidian plateau and vanishes within it. The plateau turns to liquid. A midnight oil ocean reflecting the moon and the stars and the Sky Jaws. We drop, sloshing, sinking, liquid mountain filling our eyes, ears, nose, mouth, skin, hair. Black velvet mountain-ocean in our lungs. In our blood. Pumping through our heart.

Eyes open, air bubbling, vision blurred, gaining focus. In the distance, burning horizons. Around us are hills and valleys, a few buildings (Castle Nothing), cities, worlds, catacombs. Sinking with our slow-motion mountain friends (still somewhat dancing), below us, there is an artist's rendition of what rockets *should* be. A bright smattering of sleek curves both "retro" and "future." A million versions of space travel, and the Sky Jaws refugees have embraced the vision, the concept of being completely beyond everything.

Through the mountain, beyond the buildings, there is a complicated network of train lines. There are ancient tree-skeletons, the great-grandfathers of the bone orchard infants. Off in the far away distance of our eyes, a shimmering speck of a giant construction that could only be the Orphanarium.

We sink into the Neon Rockets, passing through their exoskeletons as simply as we sunk into the mountain. Inside is the warm embrace of amber tinted air. A gentle hug to send us into space. A control panel made out of tree growth. Limbs reaching and crooked and showing a million ways to steer the ship, with no set way to do it wrong. Inside this rocket is Bullet-Boy, sitting on a luminous seat of mossy growth. Platinum has already found his seat. Vines secure us from tumbling over. Violent rumbling lets us know the rockets are ready. Are we ready, Dil?

BULLET-BOY VERSUS THE BULLETPROOF CHILD CHAPTER

The Neon Rockets have filled up with refugees. Through the body of our rocket, a familiar face. The Bulletproof Child comes here to join us on this voyage.

Bullet-Boy smiles at the newcomer and says, "I'm so glad you could be here to send us off."

Bullet-Boy sparks alight, gunpowder bursting, fragmenting his skull.

The Bulletproof Child rushes in and holds the limp body as it slumps into the ground.

The head shotguns off through the Neon Rocket,
splitting and increasing velocity
and splitting and increasing.

The Bulletproof Child is a magnet for Bullet-Boy's shrapnel.

His body is a lead balloon.

He drinks in the metal skull fragments, keeping them from flying off into the other refugees.

The gunshot starts the rocket on its skyward propulsion. The Bulletproof Child clutches on to Bullet-Boy, brings his body back home.

CHAPTER GOING INTO THE SKY JAWS

We are launched into the Sky Jaws. Neon rockets crammed with apocalyptic refugees on the long wait back home. Big ships firing lasers. Sky Jaws gaping overhead. The threat of being consumed growing by the moment. Into the wild sky, with moons buried beneath our feet.

Eyes closed for just one moment.
Just one moment.

The Sky Jaws expands and collapses all around us. Chomping at our neon tails. Storms whip the sky.
Big gushing winds and violent whirlpool rains. Turbulent rockets enveloped in dark clouds, shutting out the glitter of the Sky Jaws. A sparkling maw disappearing in the mist. Lights out in the neon rockets. We are darkness. We are silence in a wind-howling gravity storm. Wind-howling extremities in our ears. Bullet-Boy is slumped at the controls, dead before the war had a chance to kill him. He's had enough. He's coming home. There will be no rejection this time.
A swelling in our pocket, mist cloud growing, consuming the moisture in the neon rocket atmosphere. We put our hand in our pocket and the mist cloud seeps out.

There is something in the atmosphere.

A flash of little lightning from the growing cloud. A little flash and the cabin lights up long enough to see we are all okay, just floored, flung about the cabin in the chaos. More lightning and the clouds up ahead are parting to an upside down sky world ocean we shoot towards.

Rocket boosters fail. Storm dissipates. Almost at the world in the Sky Jaws, the giant star-system mouth closes behind us. No power means plummeting. The gravity of rockets falling. The gravity of passenger bombs. Falling away from the inverted liquid world in our northern vision. Slipping away from us. Falling back to our own world, back through the sky now cleared of storm, the Sky Jaws sealed shut and our own world lost from us. Wondering what will happen to us when we collide with the sky below, the Sky Jaws parts for us to collide with our own Earth. Sinking, speeding, burning, screaming, bones rattling, and a giant rain-slick hand comes out of the ground above us, below us, before us, moving through us, and we plummet into a wormhole ocean, flooding our way into the big liquid world in the sky.

THE BIG LIQUID WAR CHAPTER

Waves rip through us with such velocity, I think our bones will turn into pulp. We are on some form of transparent ocean floor. Around us the corpses of the neon rockets giving off a dull glow, a small fraction of their vintage prime. We are all dislocated in the middle of an agitated soup. People dying, people drowning, people floating up like ghosts, suffocating on the surface air. Sky Jaws Elementals swimming around us, making a killing. Swimming around us, a fleet of orphan soldiers who have been here we don't know how long, firing rockets that rip through the ocean, making it bleed. In the blossoming blood cloud, hands reach out and grab our hands and pull us to other places.

Everywhere mayhem.

Skypool Giant in the Sky Jaws, of the Sky Jaws, throws torpedos from his fists. He churns the water with his mouth, makes a whirlpool with his lips. The clouds of blood are sucked into his vortex. The dead bodies are pulled apart in the churning, disintegrating until only bones remain. The rest of the neon rocket crew have blasted through the blood bloom, the underwater fog, and are fighting against the Elementals and the orphans. It is unclear who is who is who. Elementals behaving just like orphans, just like us, and orphans with Elemental powers. The crew from Vanishing Mountain seem to exist in both worlds.

The mutant doppelganger bodies of Vanishing Mountain adapt swiftly to the conditions of the Sky Jaws. In a way, it was in their genetic material all these years. All these children exploding the children of their common ancestors.

The orphans destroying civilisations like the Orphanarium has been/is being/will be destroyed. The blood-bloom clouds bigger in the newly mixed blood before it settles and the cloud drifts out. Six tight arms grip our torso, pinning us to the ocean floor in what we understand to be some form of golden city in the middle of the ocean. Around us, people in their homes are killing and being killed. Through the glass floor, head pounding, tight chest, eyes blurring, lungs burning, through the glass floor there are more of these golden buildings just floating in the under-ocean.

We sink, dissolve, choke, vomit jetstreams of bloody water. Emerge in a strange chamber. Six arms loosen, the pressure crushing our chest relieves, and the hands pull us up. The Bulletproof Child dragged through mutated spaces, spooking us with his freakish limbs.

CHAPTER OF THE SECOND CHILD

The Bulletproof Child introduces us to his new friend.

She is an Elemental hydromancer. A student of liquid wizardry. She is kind of small, but has a fluid presence about her that feels gigantic. Her tentacles climb out of a non-dimensional hole in her back and whip through the water like bullets. Her eyes are giant black stones rolling over her skin like magnetic marbles. Rolling round her head and down her neck. One eye rolls down her arm to her palm and she brings her hands together and passes it across. All this while her blank face penetrates us with its melancholic gaze.

She is Pacifica.

She bursts open the chamber doors with her tentacles. Enters the streets of crumbling buildings and war victims bleeding out. The ocean barrier keeping one space from another is disrupted by a sonic boom. Then another. A shockwave pulsing through the water, bringing the war to a temporary standstill. There is no rage to match the one separated by this barrier. We follow the Bulletproof Child, follow Pacifica, our saviour, out into the streets turned battlefield. Down the street, there is Platinum, glowing silver in the ocean light (suns bobbing way up on the surface), his tubular arms transformed into titanium sickles stained with the blood of his now-limbless enemies. Pacifica turns the water into shields, walls keeping the Sky Jaws fighters and the invaders apart.

The Skypool Giant strikes the barrier with his torpedo fists, the citizens of the other ocean are waiting on the other side, armed with their own weapons, dying to break through and make the ocean city crumble.

The Skypool Giant laughs and plunges his fists into the barrier. He moves the water with his mind, challenging her.

She rolls her eyes, turns to us and says, "I need to take care of this. I'll come find you once I'm done." She moves through the water like a hologram speeding, tentacles tearing apart her father's face, her hydromancy keeping him from fighting back. Each generation determined to destroy the other.

She makes glass boats for us and sends us to the surface.

THE TWIN DYNASTIES CHAPTER

The water is rippled, bloodied, torn. Through the glass boats the warped images of children—Platinum and Pacifica—flailing sickle arms and tentacle limbs through the water like passing through fog. Images flashing and pulsing and erupting, bursts of places other than the Sky Jaws ocean opening up before us.

Snow on the mountaintops. Ice on the water lilies in the silent lake. A father and daughter sitting in the shallows. A father and son on the shore. A father/daughter, daughter/son sleeping at the heart of the lake, drinking in the lake water and pouring out a warm glow. A golden lake. A father and two sons, two halves of the one sun, carefully carving the sand on the bank, the stones. A moat. A funnel. Leaves and twigs, bark and strands of reed. A boat floating towards the centre. A gentle world.

Out of the air came a bolt of lightning and a resounding boom of thunder. With it came the death of complacency and the birth of chaos. *Nothing ever sleeps* became the motto of the earth. The world wrapped in rings and pulled from its infinite dream cycle and plummeted into a world where the hands that create and the hands that destroy are one and the same. Life and death each other's doppelganger. The lake split into canyons and the sky crumbled into night. The world became wolves who eventually grew into mountains, and the current mountains became cities. Trees became children who cried until they fell asleep and from their sleep they pulled their hands over their feet and made silicone shoes. The world's first cyborgs.

Dusk and dawn. New horizons bringing new territory with them. Destroyed cities where the disenfranchised ancestors collide. They grow much larger than before. Their world grows smaller. They grow more tired and more violent. More prone to death. In the sky, the ghosts of Android Wizards sweep through constellations and watch over us. The fathers with their daughters and sons, the sons and daughters of their children. Families expanding. The exponential growth of life, the surge of chaos, the complexities of being. Who we are, the people who exist for a while and then stop existing. We can grant this birthright. We can indulge reality by passing through the chaos machine one at a time and coming out the other side hanged. Coming out decapitated. Coming out slaughtered. Butchered. Annihilated.

Two things plague us: the life and the death.
Two things plague us: the when and the how.
There is certainty in chaos and destruction.
That which sleeps must waken.
That which falls must rise.
That which dies must be birthed into the world.

THE CHAPTER WHERE YOU ARE BORN AGAIN

Floating to the surface in slow motion. Thinking we should be drowning but we aren't. Thinking we should be fighting but we aren't. Thinking we should be dying.

Our boats kick through the ocean and we are on the surface of the Sky Jaws with all the floating suns bobbing around with us. Floating in the mouth of this foreign place. Floating in the sky with the world above us, the Orphanarium a shimmering mass in the far off distance.

War is beneath us. The ocean looks like glass. Through it we see clearly the golden burning buildings crumbling in the Sky Jaws. Bodies float to the surface. They rise and break through and flop on the water, rubber toys held down for a long time by a large child. We float and drift and weave around the bodies and we drift and float.

Platinum is in another district of the city, sickle arms swinging violently, attacking all comers, ripping through them like water, and his body flickers through a cycle of colours bursting lasers from his face and torso, stunning his enemies. Pacifica and her dislocated eyes rolling over her as her hands form spells with which to command the ocean. Her tentacles jab and cut at the Skypool Giant. The citizens in rebellion form rivers of gushing bodies. The Skypool Giant guides the rivers like swords and Pacifica deflects them with her growing tentacles. She wraps her tentacles around her father, constricting and constricting.

She is part ocean, but right now her tentacled form overshadows her ocean mass.

She is more Kraken than anything else.

She distorts the water around them, the barrier between the twin civilisations of the one ocean, the war-torn country, and her father is thrown through it, crushed and crumbling back to the other city with the other warring half.

And everything is closed once again.

The Skypool Giant—instigator, warlord, Element of great sky fury—is banished from his own home.

From above us, from the world, a flash of flame bursts from a point and grows into a wicked dragon face soaring up to us, growing and flashing and roaring and in an instant the massive apparition bites through our boat and we vanish into the molten ash of nothing.

THE BULLETPROOF CHILD CHAPTER TWO

Everything in our field of vision is broken. A tiny planet of lizards suspended in the air, revolving and static-erupting repeatedly into other realities. Upside down buildings. People passed through the ground and reappearing segmented in other places. Everything is suspended in a hanging honey liquid, hard to breathe, hard to move. Everything is infected with a virus from the silicon monsters. Everything is collapsing and passing through various stages of irreality. Destroyed city trapped in quarantine until the virus has run its course and everything is dead or computer fried from the world's programming circuitry. This is what happens when you try to break the program.

In the middle of the storm, the all-consuming inferno turned to ash, the world repeating, coughs up new life. A pool formed at its base from the rain of a gentle mist cloud. The Bulletproof Child drops down and pulls us up. Surrounding us, there is the destroyed city with the four fathers and their sons and daughters, and sons and daughters of their children, warped through several stages of its being. The faces of Android Wizards formed out of clouds in the sky, threatening universal apocalypse.

The creatures here are more illusion than children. Unsightly descendants from the Elementals of the sky and the earth. Hiding around windows and doorways. Ripping and shredding bits of city to the ground, the adolescent ones have their way with the world. The city is their playground. The rubble is their currency. The Bulletproof Child is our protector.

THE DESTROYED CITY
CHAPTER

This is a city of no-one. A city of decay and ruin. The sprawl forming from the dust and rubble of the eternal war. The sprawl forming from columns of fire and smoke. Digital projections of castles and towers. Through the haze, it is difficult to make out the shapes of things, but the shapes that form are the adolescent Elementals who are no longer part of the war. The discarded, the used. The ones too frail and hazardous to function properly. Those with nuclear chests glowing bright with no way to control them. These are Elementals of a different kind that the others don't like to talk about. We don't have a name for them. They just exist to tear down the towers of fire and smoke, to rip stone and melt it down into puddles of hot mush.

They scream and growl and carry on like the world is ending. Like everything around them is crumbling down, like it hasn't crumbled down already in a big pile at their feet.

Our bleary vision takes time to adjust to the destroyed city, but once it does the nameless Elementals fade away like ghosts. The children who never were, in an empty city. Only the sounds remain, whipped about in the wind.

We're struggling to figure out where we are and what we're doing. We're looking for the Bulletproof Child because we know he is here somewhere. We can sense his presence. Platinum is still off fighting in the Sky Jaws with Pacifica. We can feel his limbs crawling through us, giving us confidence.

"Bulletproof Child," you call out.

We shield our eyes and mouth from the smoke, the ash,

unsure if it is real or imagined. You call out again, but hear no response. On our shaky legs, we stumble through the rubble, through the storm of smoke, columns of fire, to a faint light where soft voices mutter.

A large creature, a gnarled and crumbling beast is hunched beside a little glowing boy and a doorway. The doorway is not attached to a wall or a building, nor does it lead anywhere except to the other side where more ruins lay scattered.

"Sunchips!" you say.

He doesn't respond.

You run to him. You call to him.

Nothing.

You glance back across the city to see where the Bulletproof Child has gone. He is no longer here. You turn back to the two creatures trying to play with the doorway. You look for any sign of recognition.

Nothing.

You reach out to grab Sunchips, but your fingers fall right through. It is the orphan army all over again, existing in a different time to us.

This is Moonhorse Juggernaut and the lost child, Sunchips. Here, Moonhorse Juggernaut is teaching Sunchips how to fix a door. He screws the hinges onto the door. Sprays them with lubricant to make sure they don't squeak. He does the top one and hands the can to Sunchips to do the bottom one. Carefully, he crouches over the hinge, and sprays too much. Moonhorse Juggernaut wipes some of it away with his thumb, but it doesn't matter. It will not squeak for years.

Moonhorse Juggernaut lifts the door to the frame, one hand supporting the door perfectly in place, the other hand screwing the hinges to the frame. His finger is a screwdriver rotating freely until it ratchets tight. He swings the door on the hinges, smooth. He holds the door for Sunchips to take and to test. Sunchips swings it open and closed. It can not swing any better.

We come close to Moonhorse Juggernaut and Sunchips. We are not afraid they will see us, or what will come of it when they do. But they are too immersed in their project to notice. Moonhorse Juggernaut drills a hole out of the door for the handle. Drills a hole out of the side for the latch and a hole in the frame for it to click in to. He inserts the latch, lining it up carefully. He fades slightly, flickers. We come closer, so close we should be able to feel his breath, feel Sunchip's heat. They buzz static and hum. Holograms clinging on to a far away past.

A distant doorway.

Moonhorse Juggernaut fits the handle and swings the door closed. It clicks shut.

He turns to Sunchips and says, "What do you think?"

Sunchips opens the door and closes it, opens it and closes it again. He nods, a fiery thumbs up.

Moonhorse Juggernaut pats him on the head and tries the door for himself a couple more times. He takes the door handle off again and plays around with it. Tells Sunchips to fetch the lubricant. He sprays the latch mechanism and plays around with it some more. Lines it up a little more carefully. Fits the door handle again and it works like magic.

We walk through the Greater Elemental and the lost child and test the door for ourselves. It is smooth. So smooth. We can not tell if this was done a day or year or century ago, but it still works like brand new. Through the doorway, we find ourselves on the other side of the destroyed city. Behind us is a tower of shimmering black glass. Surrounding us are immense buildings unpopulated. We can not tell if the city has been rebuilt or if we exist in a time before it was destroyed.

Either way, the Bulletproof Child is sitting on the path, bored. He looks up and says, "Are we ready for this?" He stands up and sniffs the air. "Stay close to me."

CHAPTER WHERE ORPHANS BECOME CORPSES

Children in tattered clothes and covered in dirt flood the streets of the city. The children of gods who have abandoned them. Children of the city which spit them out into the greater world to die. The adolescent Elementals carrying with them the stench of death and the brutality of war. The survivors of past orphan armies, a few survivors of the current war, however long it has sustained itself.

An Elemental creature with big wings and six arms calls himself the Dragonfly King. The king of the destroyed city. The king of smoke and ash. He wears a crown made of black glass. He grabs an orphan child with four of his arms, child squirming, he shoves his two free hands like spears through the child's chest and splits him in half. He launches into the sky, shrieking, and drops the two halves of the child down on us. The Elementals leap into a frenzy of dismembering orphans.

Our eyes glaze over into a matrix-space of irreality. The swooping Dragonfly King and the Elementals with their arms made of crystal blades. Hammers bursting from their hearts like catapults and crushing children into walls. Some of the Elementals seem to fight each other. Fighting for the children or fighting against themselves. Some of the children fight each other. One child shoots laser beams from her chest and rips her brothers in half. Catches a few Elementals in the process.

And here we are, Dil. Standing in the middle of it all. The Bulletproof Child has already launched himself into the battle. There's no keeping up with him, and no Bulletproof Child means the first Elemental to come at us will crush our head like a spider. They will send a bomb to our feet and launch our body into outer space. They will freeze our body still and transform us into a million little crystals.

But the Bulletproof Child has not abandoned us. We are not smashed, squashed, exploded, crushed, killed. He is moving so quick from body to body and slicing them open bloody and wet on the ground. The destroyed city massacre. The place where orphans become corpses. We unleash our storm cloud weapon upon our enemies, those monsters, those men trying to kill us before we kill them, and the storm cloud is out above us all, attacking our enemies with rain like bullets.

It electrocutes the worst of them with its lightning, while the others are slaughtered by each other and by the blade of the Bulletproof Child.

From the sky, great flaming rocket jets burn, a small cluster of Android Wizards come down and land heavy on their giant machine legs. They cut through the storm cloud, and it vortex-whirls back into our hand, like a spell which is cast out and called back, a yo-yo returning.

The Android Wizards have ceramic masks on their heads, all bearing the same blank expression.

They raise their arms.
They raise their weapons.
They prepare to raze the city to the ground.

The Bulletproof Child bursts through them, sending them

scattering about the city, buildings crumbling as they collide. They wait back, watching the Bulletproof Child, as do we, as do all the orphans and Elementals in the city. The Bulletproof Child in the centre of the brawl, mutant arms poised, ready to attack. The Dragonfly King steps forward, every limb extended, blade-fingers long and menacing, click together in anticipation.

The Bulletproof Child discards the knives he had been using to slit throats, and instead he curls his palms into fists. The Dragonfly King flies at him and slices his fingers around the Bulletproof Child's arms.

They do not slice.

They only hold. The Bulletproof Child twists and breaks off one of the Dragonfly King's Arms. Grabs and breaks another. The Dragonfly King leaps into the air, flying out of the Bulletproof Child's reach. He plummets down with remaining limbs aimed at the Bulletproof Child, to dig into his head.

He is driven into the ground. The Dragonfly King slashes and slashes at the Bulletproof Child. At his head and neck and chest, scratches up and down his torso.

The Bulletproof Child grabs the Dragonfly King by the arms and punches him in the chest until he no longer moves.

He throws the king down, and the Android Wizards come crawling back. He grabs us and pulls us into one of the crumbling buildings, an old theatre. In a dark corner we hide, squeezing into the smallest possible shape we can manage. Squeezing fingers, legs, lips, eyes.

When we open our eyes, the city is gone.

We are not innocent any more. We are none of us innocent in this world. We are just a throat-slit away from death, and what becomes of it is that we do ugly things to survive. We push down the disturbing things until they are paper-thin and flammable. We cast out the horrible and embrace the pure. When the deeds are done, we kneel by the gutter and purge.

We let go of everything until we are born again pure and innocent in the mind and flesh.

THE LITTLE MOURNING CHAPTER

In the dark slums, the streets slick with bones and pieces of bodies, the light of the perpetual night shimmering off the black glass buildings, the black glass crown of the Dragonfly King. The Android Wizards gone like all they ever were, only ghosts, myths. The city is a hot mess, but the buildings remain unbroken. The glass reflecting the hot sick blood spatter that reaches up from the streets, the desperate plea of the dead yearning to return to our world again.

So close. A distant memory.

THE FRIENDLY ELEMENTAL AND ENLIGHTENMENT CHAPTER ONE

Our vision is shaky, blurry, like this memory is somewhat distorted, unreliable. With it comes a sickness. Our body shudders. The Bulletproof Child can't save us from distress. Even though we know this memory, even though we know we are immortal until it is over, nothing could have prepared us for the fear of this unseen world. Nothing could have prepared us for these dangers, the threat beyond our own immediate realities. This is a stranger's dance, an unfamiliar song carrying us down this river. Here are the rapids. The Bulletproof Child is travelling with us, but as much as he knows, he is helpless with us. He is no more in control than us. He is no more immune to this disease. The boundaries of this world are expanded forever beyond our reach. The reality of our own ignorance is a cold shock which hits harder than the loss of our brothers.

We lay down, lost, in this shapeless city, as we tune out the patterns of our breathing, the patterns of our mind, the patterns of the survivors amongst us attempting repair, the Bulletproof Child, all tuned to a different channel, as the rain comes down in tiny pebbles, little stones carrying away blood and oil. The flesh of limbs still warm.

Out of the pebbles forming a familiar figure, a lord of the old world, a god of wisdom and understanding, a master of inner peace, reflecting our image for who we truly are. Out of the crackling interference, he comes in clear, the Moonhorse Juggernaut. The puzzle in his presence is determining if what we see is a reflection of you, Dil, or a reflection of me. Whether he sees through memories to the watcher, or if his mirror is contained within the dream.

Whatever it is we have seen/are seeing/will see, it does not matter. We are lifted from the guilt which plagues our nature. The pain and suffering of knowing a war and being helpless to stop it. There is no stopping the war-scarred orphans and Elementals from trying to tear each other to pieces. There is no saving one another. There is only saving the self.

There is only acceptance and moving on.

There is only enlightenment.

CHAPTER OF THE THIRD CHILD

Moonhorse Juggernaut calls us to him and tells us the things we create are not just material things. What we create is something which has different meanings from person to person. Where one person sees structures, another sees legacy. Where some see destruction, others witness opportunity. From the rubble, Moonhorse Juggernaut forms the shape of two familiar creatures. There is the likeness of Mr. Moon and the Seahorse man.

Where you see strangers, I see my children.

He brings them together.

My legacy.

The Moon Child.

My world revolving around them. My responsibility. Creatures belonging under my protection.

The child is real. He turns his head and blinks his giant spheres at us. Two halves forming a cryptic whole. He is suddenly far younger and more innocent. Stripped of his wisdom and magic, we see him almost as his father sees him. Almost. He is a creature we will never fully understand.

Something triggers, and Moonhorse Juggernaut becomes a different creature.

What people want with stolen children in this world, I don't know, but I don't like it.

He rises to an unnatural height, sweeping us aside with his child, bringing us under his protection, and he faces the beast risen to greet him in his own battle-worn city. The Janken Father has come to engrave his own scars into the buildings of the streets.

BATTLE CHAPTER ONE

Flashes and a sonic boom. Earthquake and the city grows tighter around us. The buildings grow taller. The Moon Child has his eyes closed and his hands wiggle in motions like a conductor or a puppeteer. How his hands mimic the battle-controlling movements of his father. Is he learning or is his father's body under his spell? He swings a moment before the fist collides. He is in control. How can he do these things? Can he really do that? This small Moon Child wielding the power of a juggernaut.

The Janken Father is the father of all technology in this world, and so his strength is not a physical one. He is a tactician. From the walls of the towering buildings, dozens of android arms burst out and grapple with Moonhorse Juggernaut. The Janken Father pivots on his body and escapes the fatal blows. He escapes certain death, yet he feels the fury behind each blow. Oh, how he feels it.

What has become of the sun child?

A sad aria ringing out into the bright night of the moon family.

A wild metropolis grown as the forests grow.

As the Orphanarium has grown/is growing/will grow.

A wild metropolis crumbling as the Orphanarium has fallen/is falling/will fall.

The sky illuminates the battle, the serenade of percussion

performing itself around us. A curtain, a window, a sphere of dust pulling everything into it.

What has become of you?

They think they know each other.

They think they know the cruelty of each other, but they don't.

The Janken Father electrocutes everything around him. Moonhorse Juggernaut slams him into the ground.

What has become of the sun child?

Platinum's ship comes screaming from the Sky Jaws and breaks to pieces on impact. He appears to be whole and relatively unharmed. He watches his father, the father of androids, returned to the oblivion from where he came. Platinum glows and already he is moving on. He is an android of functionality. He knows his father knew nothing about the missing sun child, yet he also knows that wars are not won in half-measures.

RETURN TO VANISHING MOUNTAIN CHAPTER

Platinum tells us he knows where Sunchips is, but he doesn't know how to get there. He says there's no point looking for what doesn't want to be found.

Sunchips is outside this world.

There is no finding him.

We take our cloud, unfolded from our pocket and ride it with Platinum and the Bulletproof Child back to Vanishing Mountain.

Because this place is magnetic. Because it calls us by name and knows us by spirit. Because this place was left by its people in the middle of life and was left with nothing. Because there is beauty in holding light to abandoned places. Because there is death to be mourned. Because this place pulls us in, despite it being colder now than before.

Moonhorse Juggernaut and the Moon Child remain behind in their city. They infuse it with the memory of the Janken Father and the city grows big and strong and is built so rich and full of life as the Orphanarium was built.

Because the mountain knows its way, we go the way of the mountain. We return to its reflective surface, its folds of reciprocating image. It looms massive before us. Its moonlit path our guide. We are cloudborn to the mountain, and those who ride with us become our brothers. Like they always have been.

THE VANISHED CHAPTER

The cloud, our weapon, it becomes us, becomes everything around us. It fills us with storm.

How to find a child which doesn't want to be found.

I've been there before. I'm still going through it. Where are you right now?

We pass right through Vanishing Mountain. To go the way of the mountain, we disappear. No cloud around us. No world to hold us. Platinum and the Bulletproof Child are gone. Not even Sunchips is here.

A temporary relief from the war. Lifted up and away from everything. We don't know where we are or what we're doing or how we're going to get back. We float in the undefined reality while we, ourselves, have become unreal.

THE OBSERVATION CACTUS CHAPTER

We are back in the Orphanarium. Cyberia is there. You are there. I am there. I see me through your eyes and we are identical. Only a brother knows. Only a brother can tell the difference between us.

This image holds for a moment. Cyberia taking you and me by the hand into the massive wide room with pale green tinting in the air. Vines and creepers growing on the walls and hanging hundreds of metres from the ceiling. There are about a dozen suns tracking their way across the ceiling and making grinding gear noises in their slow revolutions.

Cyberia slips from this image and takes me with her. I watch myself slip away, and we return to the room transforming around us. It brings itself towards us, the cactus. Plant Boy sits on top of it, his crown of burning roses burning bright. He holds a single spine out to us and says, "this one's for you. This is not a dream or a memory. This is only experience."

We take it from him and he says, "this spine will bring you home. You will know when to use it."

CHAPTER OF
THE MOUNTAIN
RESTORATION PROJECT

We know the rules of being here and not being here. We know the gods of men and beasts will rip our world apart. We have nothing left to hold on to. Nothing around us. Just a cactus spine from a strange creature.

The creature is gone.

The cactus is gone.

Like falling down, the sensation of rushing wind. Our body approaching terminal velocity in this dark space. We approach the ground burning. We approach reality and pass through it unscathed. We form out of cloud, into a large gathering of people—orphans, Elementals, creatures not unlike ourself— and there is a giant space before us. The space of a mountain vanished. The space where everyone forgets their war and tries to make a mountain reborn.

This is the last place Sunchips was seen. The place to which the people call him back. The place to which he must return.

We can feel Sunburst's presence in the newly returned body of her father. A giant flaming human/dragon stretching from dawn to dusk so long with his wings, a day in his body stretching on so long we forget to blink, his presence is the freezing of time. Sun-Dragon rises into the sky, and he is the eternal sunrise.

He blasts a wide arc of fire, the fury of his missing child, so fragile, with nowhere to turn. We catch in his eye the truth of his knowing.

As much as this war will tear us apart, tear apart the Orphanarium, this war is not about us. This war is beyond us. This war has scooped us up like we are nothing. This war is a game. A triviality. A bad joke. A knowledge of things once warm, now sour. An emptiness flooded into this world, and the only thing filling it is fear.

Together, we can salvage what is not yet completely destroyed.

Together we can bring the mountain back and call Sunchips back into this world to save us.

CHAPTER AT THE END OF THE SPINE

We are with the world. The whole world surrounding us, around this mountain, trying to bring it back through sheer willpower alone. There is a series of crackling and popping noises coming from some place we don't know where. The earth beneath us seems to be melting beneath the weight of all of us. The sky seems to be blurring itself away from us. The Sky Jaws is a distant dream. A constellation forever away. We will bring Sunchips back. We know it. We have seen it in our future intuition, in our liquid state of dreaming.

My conscious state of being is lifted from your body. My clarity is clouded like our storm cloud swallowing us. This is the end of your cactus dream and I am losing you. I am looking down on you and you have the observation cactus spine in your fingertips.

Why can't the dream continue on?

Why can't we keep dreaming forever?

We are pulled into a whirlpool of other places, into a heightened plane of observation. We carry on as silent spectators to your life outside the Orphanarium.

Suddenly, we are so removed from you.

THE OBSERVATION CACTUS SPINE CHAPTER

We are a transcendental lens. We are an array of visions blended into one. We are more than an android's mind, more than a processor. We are a cloud of things. We are outside the plane of physical worlds, witnessing this one with keen observation.

This is what the observation cactus has to show us. Not a perspective of a memory, but the entire picture from a distance. The clarity of omnipotence. The selection of detail becoming an overwhelming experience.

We are lost outside ourself.

We are on the wall, Cyberia and I and the lizards tumbling down, still tumbling down. We are gathered around the Vanishing Mountain, calling the mountain back into this world, and with it the lost child, Sunchips. We feel each breath of each child-warrior, transformed from their past selves, the fragile things of the Orphanarium. We sense every face of every Elemental looping around the mountain, their focus, the thoughts running through their heads.

Sunburst wrapped up in the cage of her father's body.

Moonhorse Juggernaut and all his creations resonating, living statues, growing cities. The Moon Child in his combined form, and the two separate consciousnesses which make him up.

Pacifica and the Skypool Giant lashing out across the waters of the Sky Jaws at each other, dragging countless others into their whirlpool of chaos.

How everything functions seamlessly together, moving forward as a world together, we see the Android Wizards bringing an army with them across the stars.

Not everything is decipherable. Not everything is codes. But we see enough to know that this world is slowly pulling itself apart, and there is nothing that can be done to stop it.

Our vision brings us to a golden light. A connection between myths.

CHAPTER OF THE LOST CHILD

We are in a small, dark room with Sunchips alone. Like a prison outside of time and space. A prison of Elemental proportions.

We are a little hazy towards the function of our mental projections. Unsure if what we see, we know it also in our physical body down there at the mountain restoration project. Unsure if we can act upon these visions or if we have split into two separate identities.

Can we pass on the message that Sunchips is alive and well?

Can we let the others know he has been banished to the outer limits of this world?

The mountain space trembles and the liquid of its energy flickers like the mountain is trying to return to us, but it's not quite ready. So many energies working against each other. The power of Elementals calling it back is immense, and yet it seems so small, so far away. The power within the orphan soldiers is much smaller, yet we can feel it within us. In a regular world, we could move mountains. In a regular world, we could raze the oceans to the sky and build our own cities and forests using nothing but our bare hands. We feel that power.

We are inside this small, dry, burning cell with Sunchips and we are simultaneously at the mountain, knowing we can see him. We can feel his infinite heat. We can feel his infinite energy building pressure and pushing against the confines of his cell.

He does not want to be there. We can feel the energy of the Elementals around us and we know that they can see him too. They can feel him too. Sun-Dragon roars with so much fury. He transfers his energy from his giant flaming dragon body, from every scale, from the entire length of his tail, from the length of all his molten teeth, and that energy becomes the energy of his son.

Sunchips breaks free and finds himself surrounded by Android Wizards riding giant robot dragons dunked in gold.

Just like his father told him would happen.

BATTLE CHAPTER TWO

He is fury incarnate.

He is a ballistic sun.

He spins, burning bright, fireballs spitting from his body in all directions. He spits out bits of himself like burning spines with which to destroy his enemies.

The Android Wizards are quick and fierce. Their magic protects them. Their magic attempts to reign him back in. They have giant metal sheets protecting them, coated so thick with their magic they drip with spells, leaving toxic anomalies in their wake. They spread out and form a barrier through which Sunchips can't break through. He is a cornered rhino. He is an endangered species. He is a weapon to control or be controlled by the magnetic beings riding around them. Their dragons spit out balls of plasmic energy. With the backdrop of space, they become illuminated. This segment of space becomes alive with such light it draws the Android Wizards in.

Sunchips uses their magic against them. He draws them into a black hole like the one which trapped him. They are not fools. They know when to keep their distance. They know when to play it safe.

This beast is dangerous. He is the son of chaos. He pulls a few of the closest dragons into his power and brings them to oblivion. A couple of their riders, Android Wizards sitting numb in shock and awe, they too become one with oblivion.

Mostly, they survive, yet there is no trapping the sun child for a second time. He is a liberated war beast.

He considers hunting them down, but he lets them run. He heads in the direction of his earth, bringing with him the magic of the mountain.

DEATH OF THE SEAHORSE MAN CHAPTER
AND THE NEW HEIR TO CASTLE NOTHING

A large dark ring in the sky. A mountain descending. The Vanishing Mountain returning to our reality. We see it come down from all angles and impact the ground, a minor tremor, tiny earthquake rattling through the bones of all the creatures collected here. We feel it. In the distance of the bone orchard just outside the Orphanarium, we feel it. Through the lizards tumbling slow over the edge of the Orphanarium wall where I sit, scared with Cyberia for our likely death, our impossible survival, we feel it.

A figure descending in the mountain's shadow. A being of ambiguity, otherworldly dreams, a mystery which truly belongs here.

The sky lights up a thousand silver stars, shining and speeding towards us with unparalleled confidence. Not stars, minions. The glowing lights of machines and creatures sent to us under the spell of the Android Wizards. Chaos-bots with blades out and lasers targeting down upon all of us.

Elementals and orphans scatter, out into the great wild spaces of the world surrounding Vanishing Mountain. Some of them scale the mountainside. They are the first of us to come under fire, and the first of us to retaliate.

Moonhorse Juggernaut rises to his full height and throws his hammer-fists at any and all chaos-bots foolish enough to come close enough to him. Sun-Dragon spreads his wings and takes to the sky with fire.

The mystery figure which descended with the mountain has pulled a vortex out of space, sucking in the minions and trapping them there. His cloak begins to smoulder. It burns with the passion of his being. The lost child has returned. Long live the new heir to Castle Nothing.

Minions continue to rip earth and body to pieces. They shred and destroy. They blast upwards to oblivion. They attempt to clear the path for their overlords descending. In the fire and the fury, a chaos-bot sends a monolithic cannonball through the Moon Child. It tears the Seahorse Man's face away from his brother's and leaves him carrying the weight.

Moonhorse Juggernaut builds himself into a monster, a grotesque giant with cities and forests growing from his limbs, civilisations used to justify his destruction. In this moment, every remaining minion knows their future, their imminent destruction.

CHAPTER INTRODUCING THE NEW HERO: SUNCHIPS

He burns a trail down the mountain. He burns brighter than all of us. He doesn't have his father's wings or his mother's insight.

He is galactic in his own right. He folds space around him. He vanishes and reappears on the other side of the mountain. He is the king of wormholes. He is the master of black holes. He laughs at the death which they bring. He is a magnetic destroyer of matter, yet he practices his art with unparalleled precision. He opens a wormhole to bring Moonhorse Juggernaut into the sky, to rain down death to the chaos-bots. Fizzing electricity surrounds him. Fountains of pulp sprays down from the destruction, raining down on the rest of us.

Sunburst has grown up so fast. Our body looks up at his shining, hulking mass above the mountain, side-by-side Moonhorse Juggernaut, as Sun-Dragon circles round, burning the sky up orange, his molten breath hanging in the sky, sticking to the air like glue. Sun-Dragon finishes a giant loop around all of us, a giant halo in the sky protecting the mountain.

Above it and them and all of us, a giant wormhole appears in the sky, blocking out the clouds and the stars and the Sky Jaws. We have seen nothing like it.

This was not the work of Sunchips. We see the panic in his eyes, passed on to Moonhorse Juggernaut. Our body senses the danger and our voice barely penetrates the chaos of the brawl around us, a harrowing cry of retreat. We repeat the warning and those closest to us reciprocate, and those beyond them pick up the call and on and on until we all disperse.

CHAPTER OF THE GIANT ROBOT DRAGONS DUNKED IN GOLD

Sunchips disappears in a burst of flame. Sun-Dragon spirals back down to the mountain, sinking molten mass through the reflective liquid surface of the mountain's obsidian plateau. The mountain translucent reveals his shape, curdling the liquid around him, giant gobs of neon pulling off him and drifting up like the contents of a lava lamp. Moonhorse Juggernaut plummets into the side of the mountain and digs himself into it, almost instantly becoming part of it, camouflaged.

Through the wormhole in the sky, shimmering robot dragons soar down, shining their golden scales, light bursting and reflecting in every direction. These dragons are almost as large as Sun-Dragon. Our unlimited vision takes us searching for the Android Wizard masters controlling them. The androids do not ride these dragons. They were sent ahead to terrorise. Their sonic roars echo through the mountain, out into the world to the cities and the wastelands, to the outer reach of the Orphanarium.

Dozens of them spill out. This is the real war. This is the death grip of fire and teeth and claws and android magic. We fear for our lives but we know we must return to the Orphanarium as secret heroes, or we can not return at all. For the Elementals, this is their home. If the dragons destroy that, they will have nothing left to return to.

THE BULLETPROOF CHILD CHAPTER THREE

The world is an explosion stretching on so far we can see ourselves reflected in the stars. We see ourselves reflected in the night sky. We are reflected in the mountain and in the mountain captured there are all our faces. The faces of our collected lives as humanity. As orphans and Elementals and all the other creatures living here eternal. We dance magnetic around the mountain. We whip our tails to the rhythm of the warsong. We kill and are killed. We die in fire and the crushing mass of the world around us. We stretch so far even death slips right through us. It touches us so close to our heart, we feel it inside and out, golden dragons brushing so close to our death. It passes right through us and latches on to the immortal Bulletproof Child.

His black sphere face loses its sheen. As the robot dragons swim in and out of his body like it is just another pocket of space, his organs are gentle playthings, toys for the wicked machines, he is growing pale. The golden scales explode over his body like a disease, an infection crawling over him, consuming his face, contorting it from its sleek shape. The protector becoming the unprotected. The helpless. The gone.

We feel our reality slipping into an unreliable plane.

"Come back," we call out to the falling lifeless body of the Bulletproof Child.

We know it's useless. We do it anyway.

"I need you."

The one we always thought of as immortal.

In his death his memory becomes immortal. He will truly last forever. He will never return from this war. His body is consumed by the mountainside. In the wind, the golden scales which consumed him blow away. In the wind, he is a disappeared ghost.

"I need you," we whisper again, and our whispers too disappear into the wind.

Our world shrinks down so small, right down into the palm of our hand. Our world shrinks into the space where the Bulletproof Child used to be. It shrinks into the eyes of Moonhorse Juggernaut. It shrinks into the scales of the robot dragons surrounding us. It shrinks into flames and mountains, the spaces where Sunchips has appeared and disappeared and claimed the war as his own.

We bury ourselves in the blindness of this piece now missing. We mourn for our protector and our friend. On the mountain, we mourn. In the Orphanarium, in the Sky Jaws, on the warm surface of the planet and at the outer limits of space, where the Android Wizards first crafted the image of memory, we mourn.

We mourn simply because there is nothing else for us to do.

ENLIGHTENMENT
CHAPTER TWO

The slow motion killing of Bulletproof Child. Bringing him back to life in reverse. Our entire body is hollowed out and filled up with spirit. We are an entire liquid form. We are held down by its weight. We are weightless to it, liberated. We are the exploded head of the Seahorse Man. We are a city overgrown. We are the reincarnated Janken Father. We can do impossible things. We have split this world up into different stages of reality and pretended that none of it matters. Maybe it really doesn't. Maybe we're justified in believing that somewhere amongst the stars there is the Bulletproof Child living on inside a dragon's mouth. Maybe the men who once built this world have lost control and now they're afraid. They're confused. They're overwhelmed with power and they don't know what to do with it. Our fingertips tremble as we witness everything unfolding before us. An incredible scope. A flower in bloom.

We are a very small part of a very large organism. The pieces we see are so wild and out of our control we can't help but fall in love with that which we already have. That which we know and hold dear to us. Image of you in my mind. Image of Cyberia and Killy. Image of all our fleeting sacrifices. The flickering image of Sunburst, a static image constantly shifting out of focus. That which we can't have because it is beyond us. That which pulls at us until we unravel completely.

MEANWHILE IN THE SKY JAWS CHAPTER

Bodies floating on the surface. All of them look like you and me and Cyberia. They look like orphans and they look like the refugees of Vanishing Mountain. They look like all the Elementals combined into each other. The suns are bobbing on the surface, most of them cracked and leaking their light out into the ocean, leaking out over the surface, over the bodies. The suns reach their dripping tendrils of golden light towards the mouth of stars, the bodies reach their cold, lifeless fingers up towards the earth.

Where Pacifica is, we don't know. We can't find the Skypool Giant either. They are blended into some part of the world we can't see. Either fighting or getting along, we don't know. Meanwhile in the Sky Jaws the magic of the cities has come undone. Giant curling tentacles wrap around the ruins of the cities. Wrap around bodies drowned and trying to float. The bodies of cyborgs and androids rusted out and leaking like blood. There are no sudden movements. There is no collection of life here any more. Disintegration everywhere we look. The life of civilisation crumbled away to apocalypse. Ruin is the new history. A shrinking forest moving so fast towards nothing.

The space of it rumbles, becoming undone, the Sky Jaws falling apart, drifting slowly upwards slowly pulling itself apart.

CHAPTER WHERE THE ANDROID WIZARDS COME DOWN

Space holes invade the sky surrounding the world. Wormholes through which the Android Wizards come down. They grow and hover and threaten destruction on everything around them. They turn spells over in their hands and reduce buildings to sand. They whisper secrets to the air and it carries through space and strikes lightning down on innocents.

We keep searching for Pacifica and the Skypool Giant. We find nothing. We scan our vision again and come up blank. The more we search, the less we find. Perhaps the Android Wizards are blocking the full scope of our observation cactus induced delirium. We can no longer see the mountain. We can no longer see our friends. We can no longer see the Orphanarium. The dead black spaces where they used to be. A hollow void. We can't see ourself while the Android Wizards gather around the mountain, while they proceed to destroy everything around us. They are some nightmare breed of Elemental with no conscience toward any of us.

What we see continues to distort, static and black out. We continue to be limited. Our world-eyes becoming smaller no matter how much we try to see. No matter how much we try to feel out the world, to sense the power and presence of those within it. We see the Android Wizards. We see the dragons slashing golden through the night. We see the outer edges of the Sky Jaws begin to cry and we feel like shrinking into it.

The Sky Jaws seals itself off from our eyes before we are able to complete the mental image.

All that's left to see and feel and hear and know in the universe are the faces and floating bodies of the Android Wizards casting spells. They laugh and slash blades and cast out bombs over us. They cast them out like nets over us and destroy everything we know and love. They destroy everything outside our vision.

We don't know if this means we are dead. The android king and his big android face is all we see. A smooth brushed steel shape. A small bump of a nose. There is no mouth on his face, but we can see the expression behind his electric eyes so clear as though his mouth is right there. It is small, modest. It knows things but it tells no secrets. It is sealed permanently into a flat indifference, the corners tilted upwards, hinting at smugness, knowing how desperately we fear him. Watching us flee or fight in panic. Chaos. In his eyes there is the perfect reflection. The image of a world undergoing destruction. First, the Orphanarium feels the tremors as the walls threaten to come down. Then everything expands outwards. Beyond the orphans, the Elementals turn their wild powers against these alien deities.

What is there to do to save us?

Nothing.

In the android king's eyes we see reflected not just the world as it is in ruins, but also the future torn down and rebuilt with the magic within the bones which make up his frame. Riding a giant robot dragon dunked in gold, he reduces the world and its people to dust and brings it rising back up as a shining black monument to a world born over again.

We watch the nightmare Elemental future unfold, and our observation continues winding deeper into the android king's eyes, his vision filling out everything we see, and in it there is a glimpse of light which we did not see before.

The catastrophe of hopes and dreams is that they can be broken, no matter what.

SUNCHIPS AND THE MOON CHILD CHAPTER

We are in the eyes of the android king and we feel our world expanding again. Everything fills out around us, becoming whole again. The glimpse of light a hero to our world, Sunchips returning, moulding out the missing piece of the Moon Child, not quite bringing the Seahorse man back to life, but at least making things whole enough for the Moon Child to carry that weight, to move on to more important things.

He gathers the pieces of orphans and Elementals together with the Moonhorse Juggernaut, and they rebuild pieces of living things using the pieces of the dead, the pieces of burning things sprouting into larger organisms, things more powerful than they were before. All things except for the Bulletproof Child blown away, the child already beyond calling back.

Sun-Dragon fights claw to claw, wing and breath with the robot dragons. His wings beat hard and heavy, such heat rolling through the other dragons and with each beat he slowly turns them inside out and draws them closer, turns them inside out, pulling them apart and rendering their mechanisms useless. And they feel it with every breath, every movement, every shudder shaking of their wings, their claws, their tails, every master stroke of windswept fury of Sun-Dragon, they feel it.

Moonhorse Juggernaut collects androids from the orphan army. He pieces them together and with his hands he places inside the new android the spirit of the original android master, the Janken Father. The android grows into its shape, dozens of dead androids forming new life. Sunchips and Platinum help with the collecting of pieces, they help with the piecing together of him. Platinum does not recognise the shape, but when it rises he knows, this android is the Janken Father reincarnate. This is his father and the father of androids brought back to life.

All our warriors lined up, Pacifica and the Skypool Giant have returned to our vision, the Sky Jaws destroyed, homeless, they have left it to ruin, and they descend on the Android Wizards from above.

The Moon Child picks himself up and creates weapons from his surroundings, ready for battle. Sunchips creates a wormhole through which to throw the Moon Child into the fight.

BATTLE CHAPTER THREE

What results is a storm of bodies. The first rains from the Sky Jaws coming down on us through the big black swirling holes in the sky. Elementals energising each other bringing new power to their bodies and inflicting damages upon the Android Wizards.

The Janken Father rises and releases a sonic roar which resonates through the Android Wizards. It warps the space around them and distorts their technologies. The ground rumbles and the compacted earth beneath us swells with heat. Unnatural things rising up. Holograms swarming the sky and latching on to the Android Wizards and the robot dragons. Fire children latching on to their circuit boards and pulling them to pieces. Gravity tormenting them.

We conjure up our storm cloud and ride it into battle and from our fingers we shoot lightning at the distorted android warriors in the sky. They are pulled apart yet their number never thins. Their pieces are magnetically returned and they continue casting spells.

Out over the bone orchard, columns of sand fountain into the air, the mass of twisted bone trees growing and twisting and connecting and pulling themselves from the ground. This is not a bone orchard, it is a bone *cemetery*. Hundreds of millions of orphans dead and buried in the sand, bones connecting and rising, this is where the orphans go to die. This is where they come when they are past their years. Now the remains form an army of bone-lizards, whipping tails and sharpening claws, ripping chunks of metal from the earth to make their armour, pulling robot parts up through the sand to transform themselves into skeletal cyborgs.

The Android Wizards and robot dragons descend on them. They descend upon the mountain and on the Orphanarium. They descend on Castle Nothing, peel back the roof and are met with explosive fire. They sling lasers from afar. They ride their dragons through wormholes and come out in other places. Giant wet hands crush them to the earth, fire reduces them to ash, android and cyborg warriors scramble the war into a virus, fighting lasers with lasers and magic with unseen powers. The gravity of all of this is indecipherable. Lights and energy, blades and guns throwing projectiles in every direction.

This world will make killers out of us all.

THE DRAGON
AND ELEMENTAL
SHOWDOWN CHAPTER

The pieces of blown apart robot dragons come together, forming out of them a bigger dragon to tear through the Elementals. It is far bigger than us. It shadows over the mountain and threatens to wipe all of us out completely. Crawling over its body there are thousands of blades revolving, slashing through the air, forming golden limbs to reach and cut us into pieces.

The Android Wizards stand on the back of it and cast their spells, throwing knives and bombs and lasers, throwing black holes and wormholes. They gather around the android king and become part of him.

Moonhorse Juggernaut becomes the skeleton of a warrior. The Janken Father becomes the energy to his body, Sun-Dragon sets his flaming body down on the massive stone back, wings to give flight, a molten throat to blow fire on their enemies. The Skypool Giant wraps his big wet arms around the growing figure.

The collective World Elemental crouches atop Vanishing Mountain, the obsidian plateau reflecting its menace. It pounces into the sky and grips the golden dragon with its Skypool arms, golden blades harmlessly slashing at water. An electrified tail slashes at the dragon limbs. The Sun-Dragon head bites chunks off the robot dragon and fills its insides with white hot fire.

The children combine and launch onto the dragon's back, advancing upon the android king. The remaining Elementals and orphans gather into battle formation and the Vanishing Mountain begins to glow and hum, machines within it spinning and pulsing, liberating the warriors from their gravity. You float with them, with your cloud soaring around the dragon.

From the fringes, the skeletal cyborgs emerge, floating, flying, penetrating their sharp bodies into the golden armour with fury.

THE BROKEN SKY
JAWS CHAPTER
AND THE FLOOD

The Sky Jaws continues to rain its leaking ocean, and the ocean itself slides towards the mouth.

Sunchips sends a shooting star up into it. We watch the Sky Jaws burst apart. The rain turns into a flood, an entire ocean falling from the sky.

The catastrophe of events surrounding us, the giant golden dragon smashing things and being smashed by the World Elemental and by the Elemental children, the skeleton cyborgs, all the creatures living and dead fighting the giant robot dragon and the android king, pulling them to pieces as the avalanche of ocean comes down, the giant creatures split apart and disappear in all directions, but they never really truly disappear.

Platinum stabs them, the Moon Child smashes, Pacifica uses her hydromancy to rip her enemies in two. Sunchips creates a whirlwind of black holes with which to seal away the Android Wizards and the robot dragons dunked in gold.

The flood comes crashing down, washes through the world, giving us time to breathe and think and return to our feet. The skeletal cyborgs dig themselves into the ground. All the orphans and Elementals, holograms, Android Wizards and dragons—we are all of us drenched and at a loss for what to do. What we might call a stalemate. One world destroying another over and over, neither conceding defeat.

The ocean soaks into the earth and begins building forests full of mountains and cities. A dark space within a mystery cluster of trees. Life perpetuating, fleeting and returning, combing through the earth and the clouds. Life recedes, and life returns.

We see you climbing high in the clouds, owning them, embracing your fate as a warrior. And as your cloud soars above all the others, reaching its apex, your euphoria is frozen by the blade of a golden knife pricking the skin on your neck.

THE SKY WAR CHAPTER
(AKA CHAPTER OF THE ELDER ELEMENTALS)

Everything is segmented into quarters and all the friends and enemies unleash their powers. The sky is a battlefield. There is an ocean of water Elementals in the sky. There is a constellation of Elementals descended from the stars, descendants of fire. There are the natural satellites, the moons and asteroids, the rock Elementals, breaking apart everything around them. And there are the orphans, the androids, the Janken Father. The Elder Elementals, the giant warriors of the sky smashing up a series of fireworks.

Suspended above the clouds, there we are. With a knife held firm to our neck, there we are. Only a moment, and then the knife tumbles back down to earth. The hand which held it falls to the Android Wizard's side, and in our omnipotence, we witness the blade splitting through the Android Wizard's skull. Feel the magic leaking from him, dripping through clouds.

Everything in this world is a dream of blood and adrenaline, wars between life and death. We roll through the sky, cloud-burning a trail of ash, ignited by an Android Wizard possessed by the spirit of the sun. We are instantly extinguished and we soar on. We have Platinum with us, slashing with glass blades and mapping our path out with his mind monitor. He is connected to the Janken Father, and we feel the connection too. Everything channelling into the one path.

There is no victory. Only destruction.

There is no war. Only annihilation.

Us or them, we don't know. All we know right now is a vision fading and a magnetic force pulling us back home.

The android king is destroyed by the children of the Elder Elementals converging where the four quarters meet. Platinum's bloody blades would help us return to the Orphanarium, but his absence on our cloud can not be avoided. His blades and the destructive forces of his Elemental siblings dissolve the barriers.

The warriors touch ground. We know it. We're done.

CHAPTER WHERE YOU RIDE THE STORM CLOUD

Before we realise where we are, before our vision can zero in on our location, we can feel the cool breeze through our skin. We're chasing home. We're fleeing a war that is far beyond us. We're fleeing something infinite, something terrible, and while we flee, we know it is something we can not escape forever. We leave Platinum and Pacifica, the Moon Child and Sunchips to fight their war. We leave them to sift through the remains and try to make sense of it all. What home remains for them now. We ride our storm cloud through the clusters of warriors floating and drowning and fighting and bleeding out. We ride our storm cloud out over the landscape now mutated, a ghastly transformation of what once was, and everything around us is changing, crashing down or rising up or latching on to things and bringing them into the new landscape.

The king is dead and the war is trapped for the moment in a violent slow motion which we have temporarily escaped.

Every moment on the cloud is spent expecting everything to catch up to us and consume us.

Every moment is spent fearing change, knowing that change is the only way forward.

To stay the same is suicide.

ENLIGHTENMENT: THE FINAL CHAPTER

The peace never stays for long. It never does.

We are lost in the dream state of observation. Death and danger and an ocean of calm.

Inside the Orphanarium with the Cyborg Lizards, the panic and the chaos. On the wall outside the Orphanarium, watching myself and Cyberia and the waterfall of lizards in slow motion.

We are invisible. We are removed from everything at the same time as we are completely immersed in it. You and I existing in this vacuumless non-space, our world happening all around us.

I am wondering, have been wondering for a while if you have been running some form of autopilot program inside your body while your consciousness has been torn from it. I am wondering if you can still control yourself from the distance of the observation cactus spine.

You are on your storm cloud, creating the rain and thunder and wind that throws the war into a state of confusion. A state of rage. A blind fury that transcends simple emotion and brain chemicals. You are perfectly wounded from the death of the Bulletproof Child. You fight the Android Wizards. Their lasers melt with your lightning and form molten fury exploding through the sky like a star bursting into oblivion. The steam and monsters, men and Elemental warriors fighting anyone and everyone. The sky melting. In the chaos there is calm.

Moonhorse Juggernaut has remade the body of the bulletproof child, that immortal skin, and he holds it into the air and you swoop down, and the storm cloud absorbs his mass, absorbs his power.

Barriers are torn down and barriers are resurrected.

Those who wish to fight, stay and fight. Those who wish for peace make their exits. The flurry of bodies and weapons. The mass of warzone splits in two. It shifts from an infinite space to a finite space. It splits again, and again. A million times over. Those who wish to die present themselves for the taking. Those who wish to kill find themselves scrambling like madmen. In the rapid sprawl of warzone rendered finite, collapsing and splitting and rapidly returning to the complexities of infinite warriors, there is you on a storm cloud retreating, embracing eternity and enlightenment.

All the people you ever knew are eternal.

All the people you ever loved are infinite.

All the people you ever lost are immortal.

RETURN OF THE ORPHANARIUM CHAPTER AND THE BULLETPROOF CHILD MEMORIAL

There you are, riding on your storm cloud through a kaleidoscopic warzone.

Beneath you on the desert floor, Moonhorse Juggernaut turns timber and stone over in his hands, putting together a new design while he has a dagger sticking out of his neck and half his chest is missing like something has eaten or smashed it away.

A giant golden robot dragon swoops in from your side.

In this moment you are immortal.

You leap into the sky.

The dragon swallows your storm cloud and you grab the dragon by its fiery gemstone horns.

Dipping low, it spirals rapidly, electronic roar blasting through the air, plummeting to the ground with the sole purpose of destroying you.

Moonhorse Juggernaut throws a boulder at the dragon and decapitates it.

Golden scrap metal raining down, disintegrated. Bucked off, lacerated palms, your storm cloud scoops you up from the dismantled beast and puts everything behind you.

The flood, the steam and monsters from the Sky Jaws, the Android Wizards, the children and the battling Elementals shrink into the distance.

This is not your war any more.

This is a world dismantling itself, a world beyond repair.

Up ahead, on the wall, there I am with Cyberia and the avalanche of raging lizards.

In the desert of the earth, there is Moonhorse Juggernaut with his large, calloused hands, carving out a memorial statue, a living statue of bone and mortar, organs of sand and water, of sun and moon and earth and steam. A memorial for the death of the Bulletproof Child, his body draped in the piecemeal armour of giant robot dragons dunked in gold.

In our memories we are immortal.

Return to the waking world, to your home with no furniture. With war paintings on the walls. With a Sky Jaws carved into your ceiling. A paintbrush of your memories.

You left the war behind, Dil, but you never let it slip from your memory. You brought the war home and made it your life. Your immortal war forever repeating beneath your skin. You brought the war to me.

"So now you've seen it too?" a gentle voice from the shadows. A dull orange glow. Cyberia steps out. Killy in her shadow.

I nod.

In this war we are immortal. We are connected. We are numb. We are dead.

Chaos is the language of our people.

Self-destruction is the only exit.

BEYOND

CHAPTER SET IN THE CHURCH OF THE BROTHERS OF MEMORY

This place doesn't feel any safer. Through the emptiness of this home we know you will never return here. You have gone through hell, willingly, knowingly, you entered the vicious cycle. You knew us and loved us and saved our lives. Helped us save each other, only to drag us into it too.

These things which can't be forgiven.

These things which circulate in our nightmares.

You gave me your war story. You gave it to Cyberia too. You left us to our own devices, wondering why you called us here, to see your place like this, to see and feel and know exactly what you've been through, only to find you had rendered yourself invisible.

What ghostly apparitions could tell us the meaning of this?

We turned your place inside out in search of something, anything which might indicate where you were going or what you were doing. To locate you in the present, we studied all your drawings on the walls and ceilings. We combed through every room and flipped each phantom mattress. We turned your home inside out and came up empty. When we were done, we did it again. When we were done, we peeled back the wallpaper and pried up the floorboards.

We took a break and stuck the warbound needle in our skin again. We remembered your repeating brush with death, your fleeting moment in the outside world, the rush of life and catastrophe. Never getting any closer, only driving ourselves mad with the puzzle. We become lost as we were sure you too were lost.

When we were about to burn your home to the ground, giving up and cutting off all ties, two lizard men in uniforms like I'd never seen, they came and caught us match-in-hand and took us away. They brought us to the church of the brothers of memory. They took us right to you, and now we see what has kept you so busy while we had gone our separate paths.

THE CYBERIA/CINEMA CHAPTER

In this church, there are long, open hallways draped with tapestries, images painted on them of the detailed scenes of your time at war. A monument to your heroism. A monument to the death of the Sky Jaws and the death of Bulletproof Child. The Seahorse Man. The android king. Golden dragons on the tapestries flying from wall to wall. The burning brilliance of Sunchips and Sun-Dragon, the enigmatic absence of Sunburst. She has come back, is coming back, will come back, and her life will not be lost. It will not be for nothing.

There are secret rooms with big heavy holographic doors humming electric, through which only the occult members of the church pass through to their secret meetings. We pass through one hallway, out into a space far wider and taller than before. It feels like we are out in the open space of the Orphanarium, the giant rooms dwarfing everything around them. But this is an entire space of it that is reserved for the church. It serves no other purpose, and Cyberia and I walk through the room, the grey/green tinting in the air, the church lizards guiding us along a stone path, past countless creatures kneeling in front of processing screens, processing their prayers.

Such a long stretch to the other side of the room, where there is an incredible staircase stretching many times as wide as it is high. At the centre, at the top, there you sit, a gaunt clone of the brother I once knew. Cyborg arm a clone of the one you used to have. And there, by your side, sitting cross-legged on the floor, is Cyberia. Not the age-worn android who came with me here, but a pristine clone—a literal clone—of her, so bright and smooth and silent. A needle in her skin, the vacant gaze of a mind in memory. A plug latching on to the back of her head, pulsing light and sucking that part of her away.

You hold a finger to your lips for quiet, and point at the wall behind you. It illuminates an image in the Orphanarium, a space which we are unfamiliar, and the lizards bring us chairs to sit and watch the film, the vision, along with all the others in this room on their prayer screens, along with you, Dil, watching the screen as it hovers that exact same image in the air out above the stairs in front of you.

THE FIRST VISION
CHAPTER

A blazing sun. Outside the Orphanarium there is a blazing sun hanging in the sky, encased in glass, smiling down on us. A vision of warm auras. Like the entire contents of Castle Nothing, the sun families combined in galactic radiance. And there is the earth of red sand, not the colour of rust or ochre, but the full rich red colour of blood. Monuments erected from the sand, sprawling figures dynamic, so real-looking they are intimidating. Cities formed out of stone and steel, twisting and growing into sleek, flat platforms of polished black stone from which their foundations are formed. There is the Orphanarium built up larger and more impressive than any civilisation around. The pillars of Elementals are terrifying as they are beautiful, but we are part of something, the magnitude of which is completely unreal. The screen closes in on the Orphanarium and the outer walls are crawling with skeletal cyborgs. They are crawling with fire demons, and their claws and teeth pull at the outer bits of the skin of this place and the vision cuts out to a room full of silence, like all the voices within it have been evaporated. Like the sound waves have been absorbed into the walls.

The war is never over. You have your own following now, more a cult or an army than a church. You have your own Cyberia. She lives to inject these memories, to transmit them out to your people. The throne to this kingdom is yours.

How much of it is truly yours?

CACTUS PLANTATION CHAPTER

We stand on a balcony overlooking a giant room. You, me, the two Cyberias—and now I wonder which one is the true version of her, the sparks crawling down Killy's electric spine an indicator—and the room is wall to wall rolling fields of cactus plants. Creatures down below ploughing the fields, harvesting and watering the cactus seeds. The first seed which you plucked from the ashes of the World Cactus. You cloned it and modified it in the android markets, just like you cloned and modified Cyberia.

This is your cactus plantation, your endless supply of vision and memory. The oracle of this city, you will lead it to ruin or prosperity. There is no middle ground, and you know this. This is your inevitable fate, as was the war, as was the inevitability of its continuation towards ruin, your inability to stop it.

CHAPTER OF THE PLANT-MEN

Instead of polished concrete or steel beneath our feet, there is sand. The dry sand of deserts on the plantation floor. Here we are. Through the plantation we move. Tending to the cacti, harvesting their seeds, there are creatures of the Orphanarium like nothing I've seen before.

Lies.

They are somewhat like the Elemental who burned down the World Cactus, the one with a crown of burning roses round his head. Plant-Boy. These are plant-men. Bigger bodies of tree-brown bark-muscle. Their eyes stare yellow into ours as we pass them. Plant-Boy was more foliage than tree, yet these men are of the same kind, the same earthy tones in their sap-filled bones, beneath a skin of photosynthesis.

You have done it again. Mutations and clones. Your attempt to replicate and control. An ever repeating cycle which will end in deadly paralysis. A world overfilled with clones there is no space left to move or breathe.

The plantation sits on a complex network of pulleys and discs, each one controlling a different part, a different mechanism spinning or shifting a different batch of cactus to a different part of the room. The tinting in the air is split by prisms forming invisible barriers. The plant-men move them around as needed. They adjust the brightness of the suns, the angle, the quality of their light. The suns hang relatively low in the room, considering the scale of the ceiling stretching out so high.

Far above the suns, there are big ships hanging on steel cables slowly moving overhead and even though we lack the precision of Cyberia's telescopic vision, we can see that these are not cargo ships, but passenger ships. The people of the church coming and going from the screen room to other parts of the church, perhaps even other parts of the Orphanarium. Even after seeing this place from the outside, we have no idea how big this place actually is. An image beyond conception.

Beyond the ships, still, the unmistakeable markings, distinct pattern of stars in the sky, perhaps a mural or a replica of the water world suspended in space, the Sky Jaws.

THE NEW BROTHER CHAPTER

"What happened to you?" Cyberia asks. This is the Cyberia which came with me.

You shrug and turn away. "War happened. Shit, life happened. Time happened. Continues to happen. Do you know how much the outside world has changed since we returned? Hell, do you know how much has changed since you saw what I saw, since my people brought you here?"

Cyberia says nothing. Neither of us do.

You speak for us. "Too fucking much."

Cyberia is right. You're right, too, of course. But Cyberia is right in thinking something doesn't quite sit right any more. We're brothers. Twins. And now it seems like you have more in common with the new Cyberia than you do with either of us. The words hang like apparitions just beyond our field of vision. Ghosts, clones, shells of what once was. Like maybe the rest of you remained outside in the rain and war. But that's not right either. It seems more like you've been reborn, baptised by the new religion which compels you. The destiny for all of us to drift apart.

Are you the same brother who was born from the Orphanarium with me? Were you the one who came with me into being, from nothingness, emerging from the vacuum of space into orphanhood. You may be a clone, we don't know. You may have transformed from your former self. All we can do is take you as you are and hope some day you return to recognising our connection.

As a fact, you have been cloned. There is another clone sharing our identity.

We are in a projection room—one of dozens, you tell us—and Killy lets out a sonic growl. There you are again, replicated and strapped down to a chair. Your clone an empty shell. A vessel through which the images pass. Sterile creatures move about the room religiously sacrificing a cactus spine into the skin of your other self. They plug him in to a network of screens and on the countless screens in the compact room we see what he sees, the image set to broadcast throughout the church.

THE CLONE SCREENS CHAPTER

On the screens, there is a hyper-saturation of tinting in the air. Violet. The night sector in MLO with the sprawling towers twisting into spires like giant conical shells. Conveyor belts pass from tower to tower; thousands of silver tokens on the silent belts, sleeping. The floor is a black silicon grid. High above, looking out over all the towers, the image hangs. For minutes passing we watch the sleeping coins lie in silence.

Then, a faint rattling, rumbling. Like something far away is shaking the foundations of the building. It builds up a little, then it stops. It starts again, then grows faint, moving away. You shake your head and one of the projection room technicians rips the spine out and tosses it into an overflowing bin. We leave your numb, hollow self to its endless dream-state, harvesting spines, and into another, almost identical room we go.

All those abandoned spines. None of them good enough. The distant rumbling an insignificant dream. What giant monster moves within the Orphanarium? Or what monster outside the Orphanarium could be so heavy to shake the foundations so deep, to reach into this building so far that it can be felt even in the night sector?

You see the thoughts revolving in my head as you place your young Cyberia into the vacant screen-seat. She shivers with excitement, ready for that cactus dream-state high.

"Don't think there's only one night sector any more," you say.

In this room, there are no spine bins. Only rows and rows of spines sitting bloody in test tubes. You take a spine and sink it into the blood-black hole in Cyberia's arm, the hole which has been subject to so much abuse, memories repeating all over again, projected out to all your followers. The visions you want them to see.

"As much as the outside world has changed, brother, things have changed in here too."

Cyberia's monitor lights up golden and the image pops up on the screens in the room, but also transmits beyond the room. Effortlessly, this young creature of Cyberia's image, she transmits the cactus image out into the church, out into the Orphanarium.

"Did you feel it?" he asks.

The tremors. The image of the night sector. It wasn't a vision of the future or the past. It slipped right through us in the moment, while we were watching, some distant beast was moving, the Orphanarium shaking with the screen, synchronised.

THE CHAMELEON AND THE BEARDED DRAGON CHAPTER

We are inside one of the big ships moving on steel cables way up high above the cactus plantation. We move through it and gaze up at the replica Sky Jaws hanging there, a memory, a reminder of what we've seen, what you've been through. Who you are now, we don't really know. How you built this empire. How this entire sector of the Orphanarium has transformed around you.

In the Sky Jaws, a storm. The sounds of thunder and harsh rain. The flickering swell of storms deep within the mouth of stars, waiting to overflow, waiting to burst like its cosmic other.

You seem so driven by this new vision of yours, and yet nothing of what you do seems to feel right. Nothing of what you do seems to resonate the character we once knew. You have gone the way of the Sky Jaws. You used to have your own gravity, we had our own collective gravity. A destiny which held us together. And now the stars are broken and the great oceans of you have slipped right through, so much we couldn't bring you back.

The ship we're on shuts down suddenly, everyone looking around in panic, looking for something of a cause. Lights casting shadows over all passengers, and somewhere outside the ship, the hum and whir of cyborg movements, the clunk of cyborg hands climbing around and reminding us that this place is still ruled by the cyborg lizards, Jingo Incorporated, the hostile children of the Janken father. The children plagued by the nightmares of a world spiralling out of their control.

Here come the brothers of brutality and secrets.

Here come the Chameleon and the Bearded Dragon.

And the ship moves again. And the Bearded Dragon sits opposite us. And he scratches the reptilian flesh dangling from his neck. And a metal patch is welded over his eye socket like yours, and inside it shutters open and closed a cyborg eye. And he nods at you and yours.

And the environment is hostile.

The chameleon moves throughout the ship, keeps people seated. He moves invisibly smooth, morphing his skin between states so much and so natural like breathing. His loose reptilian cloak shimmers metallic, it comes and goes. A flash of eye contact. A flicker of a forked tongue. Nimble limbs crawling, ready to sling blades, into the folds the sounds of the moving ship, gone.

THE NIGHTOPOLIS CHAPTER AND THE RAISING OF THE COINS

Through walls we pass, leaving the cactus plantation, the moving fields far below, the complex network of suns shining ship-shadows above us on the walls, on the ceiling around the Sky Jaws, swirling mobiles of shapes, ships and suns converging into the one concept.

Our ship shrinks from room to room, expanding exponentially through each one we pass. Our only constant is the thick steel cables pulling us along and the penetrating gaze of the cyborg lizard, the Bearded Dragon.

Enter the night.

Enter the sector of the damned towers filled with coins.

The air tinted thick and heavy violet, like breathing syrup deep into your lungs.

Inside the ship, a shaking. A distant tremor running through the cables. The people on the ship like Cyberia and like me, staring about wildly for the source of it. You and your clone Cyberia continue your melancholic gaze into the Bearded Dragon. Him fiercely gazing back, sharpening his claws, his teeth. His bulky head way too big for his eyes, increasing his menace tenfold. The sharp plates sticking out of his spine running up to the top of his skull an exoskeletal mohawk.

Cyberia drinks in the violet tinting and it absorbs into her face, her glowing eyes, faint colour in her lips and cheeks, electric crackling down the length of her fibre-optic hair, washing her over in new light, and washing her somewhat in calm. Your clone Cyberia remains pale, softly cycling through the rainbow on her synthetic skin.

The Chameleon flashes his white light about the ship like a sword as the tremors continue, freezing people in their seats, bathing them in calm and still. The tremors are real, only resonating in our heads as though they have been contained there.

The ship reaches its port at the Nightopolis station, sitting high above the city and its ethereal glow. Its ghostly presence is pristine, revived from its past apocalypses. The penguins exterminated from it.

From the ship, the Bearded Dragon follows us out, so close his beard of skin brushes the back of our heads. The Chameleon is ahead of us close somewhere, but he blends so well we can't see him. Through the Nightopolis we follow the shape and shadow of the Chameleon, knowing our direction is being decided for us.

There is persuasion, and then there is *persuasion*. We don't tempt fate this way.

We feel the tremors through the black silicon grid floor, we feel it stronger as we approach the towers and towers and conveyor belts of coins. The orphan sleepers. What creature rumbles and threatens to disrupt the slumber here?

In the night sector air it is hard to see, past the towers it is so dark like the spaces which have never known the gentle touch of light. Through the dark a soft red glow. Running from the ceiling down, a concrete pylon. A great beast of Elemental magnetism, red glow pulsing, rings descending. Reach the ground, releasing tremors. Swelling and receding without consistency, only announcing one message: I am here.

The mother of Cynthia, the pylon Elemental, the shape of things which take hold of our world and pull them apart with their gravity. A ring of roses, a revolution. An apocalypse of destruction remembered, repeated. This mother unleashed upon the Orphanarium with the matching name of Cynthia, too. The older, the younger, one and the same. Rings hovering and pulsing louder, brighter, hotter, faster.

This time we don't feel it. We stop back and watch. With the Chameleon and the Bearded Dragon, you, me, the Cyberias— the one with Killy in her arms and the one without.

The sound of a mechanical vortex, the winding up and power, Cynthia pulling the coins up from their towers, rattling them wild and rising up, stirring back to consciousness, the coins expand out, all of them in a chain reaction, the gravity of Elemental magic, Cynthia playing with them like toys, they return to their orphan forms and hang, floating in the space above the towers, very much awake.

THE ELEMENTAL RAID
CHAPTER

The night-light suns flicker before coming to full light, twisting and releasing from their tracks, falling, revolving, shining brighter, glass and light unravelling to the form of giant glass and light people. Like Sunburst, burning from within, radiating into the night, moving as Elementals do, but new enough to the world to not quite know where they are or what they do.

They climb the towers and tear them down. The chunks of concrete and steel which crash into the ground become unfolded into the shapes of people—like the night sector suns—they become alive. These bodies heavy with their concrete and steel mass coming alive, and follow the suns in destroying the night sector and using it in their self-replicating ways to build themselves an army. They spread out and work their way circling around, spiralling in towards the pylon, Cynthia, and towards the giant mass of awakened orphans.

From the black polished mirror-wall at the far end of the night sector, more creatures come. Around us the creatures of light and glass, concrete and steel move like we're invisible. From the far end of the night sector the shapes of distant monsters come into clarity and we see them from the vision of the Orphanarium outside being torn apart. They found their way inside just like we went outside—through the cracks they came.

Here are the wild beasts of bones and cyborg scrap. Wild bone warriors, wild beasts with fire demons on their backs, riding them into night and pulling it into chaos. With their sharp claw feet, the skeletal creatures pull up chunks of the black silicon grid flooring, each chunk roughly the size of us, each chunk unfolding into a person and running alongside or riding with the beasts to the towers to pull them all apart.

One skeletal cyborg rushes at the base of a tower and charges right through it, big and unrelenting, uproots it like a tree falling down sideways. The tower picks itself up monolithic and shaped intimidating like an upside-down mountain with a series of giant fists ready to tear the Orphanarium apart room by room.

With the Bearded Dragon and Chameleon we watch the chaos around us, we watch the night sector crumble to pieces and pick itself back up.

CHAPTER OF THE PULLING OF THE WALLS

"There is no stopping this," you say.

Black silicon people running past us towards the Nightopolis.

"You need to watch this," you say.

The creatures of destruction continue pulling apart the floor. Where there should be an opening in the floor, in the ceiling of the room below us, there is nothing but the image of a deep black well. The texture when we walk over it is hot sand, blistering. The creatures crawl over the walls, pull the mirror wall reflection to bits, crawling on the ceiling pulling their way higher, up and out.

Freedom for all.

Space for all.

Long live the Orphanarium.

Watch it burn.

And from the ashes, rise.

You stab your Cyberia with a spine and her head rolls back. You hold it still. She is a slave to this process. She embraces it.
    "Watch."
    Her crystal mind monitor shines up and projects a

hologram screen out for us to watch. On the outside of the Orphanarium, the Elementals pulling at the cracks. Making them bigger. Pulling the walls to smaller pieces. Working their way through the roof, through the floor, the walls, through the cracks. The children of their manifestation claiming this world and pulling apart everything in their way to return. The climb from night sector to the outside. The climb from the outside in. It all means inevitable collapse. It means disintegration. Everything here has become ripe for the harvest. They have come to collect on their investment. They will leave nothing for us.

"See?" you say.

THE SECOND VISION CHAPTER

You take the spine out and replace it with another. "Soon," you say. This vision will happen soon.

Image of a body nailed to the wall of the church up high for everyone to see. What everything comes down to, this body with thousands of long, sharp spines sticking right through it, holding it up. A porcupine from the outside in. This body is you. It is your body drained of its blood, of its memories leaking red down the wall in long, skinny dribbles.

Tough gig.

What cacophony of images spill from the myriad spines in you, we don't know. Only you know in the dying. In the vast chamber of your church, empty and crumbling, only you holding steady up there on the wall

Only you know the reality of this situation. Only drowned in memories you know. Leaving Cyberia and I to wonder if this version of you is real, or just another replica. A shape formed in your image.

The shape of things to come, vague and violent.

We leave the night sector before it swallows us whole. We follow the Bearded Dragon lumbering giant out of here, the shape of the Chameleon keeps us in line. I'm not sure if they are protecting us, or if they are making sure we don't disturb the order of things, the progression towards destruction. Your death is already a given. What is there to lose from here on out?

CHAPTER OF THE FALLEN SKY JAWS

Simultaneous images, a legitimate memory calling, not from the psychosis of sharp objects jabbed into our skin. What it looks like when the Sky Jaws has replicated itself inside our world. What it looks like when the replica spews deserts of red sand from its twinkling mouth. The mouth of the Sky Jaws outside, hollowed out of its oceans, I remember the image. The homes of water-dwelling space creatures, destroyed. Our red earth flooded and then dried up.

Our Orphanarium flooding with an ocean of sand. The sand of the outside world flooding in. Flooding the cactus plantation. Flooding down over the ships and cables, down over the suns, down. A desert for the cacti. A desert spilling out into other places. Heat swelling and rising and bringing all the lizards up and out. Watching the lizards rise. The Bearded Dragon and the Chameleon remain with us in the disarray, as hundreds of Plant-Men scatter, as we catch fleeting glimpses of orphans and Elementals and decipher how much of what we see is illusion.

The Bearded Dragon bursts open the steel door to the church, already filling up with sand. All around there are screens with people watching them, watching the outside of the Orphanarium full of holes and cracks through which the Elementals flood in. The desert surrounding the Orphanarium sinks or perhaps the entire building rises up. The concrete pylons which anchor us into the ground becomes pulled up and the Orphanarium is uprooted from its foundations. Before long, there are very few Elementals left outside the Orphanarium. The building has grown itself outward to consume more of the space outside. To accommodate for the Elemental population within.

You know these creatures. You've fought wars beside them.

How do we fool our memories into thinking we can survive? How do we outlive our brothers and sisters while the world around us is dying? When the Elementals themselves seek refuge within these walls? When they bring oceans and deserts, cities and suns with them, what do we do then?

THE GUARDIAN'S WAR CHAPTER

We watch the visions flicker and cycle through images schizophrenic.

Janken Father and the Moonhorse Juggernaut, the original cyborg and the original architect. Moon and robot, flesh and power. Combining and patching up the walls. Holding us together.

Killy shakes so fearful in Cyberia's arms. She pops and fizzes. She disappears and reappears, flickers in and out of space while we watch the screens do the same, concentrating on the broadcast.

Castle Nothing contained within the Orphanarium. A giant cavern surrounding it, hollow and wet. Empty. The familiar landscape of the Destroyed City rebuilt, now sprawling across the walls and ceiling. A giant ocean contained within a glass sphere, a former Sky Jaws retained in its own world. A Skypool Giant, a Pacifica. Revolving around them, a Sun-Dragon bursting his way into death and from the wash of light, Sunburst reborn. Sunchips is already discovering other parts of the Orphanarium.

These new sectors which have no name. The Orphanarium being simultaneously created and destroyed. The Elementals are our guardians and our enemies. They tear us down and build us back up. The never-ending war.

The Orphanarium is expanding into the greater world and we can not hold it. We can not contain it. It will consume everything as it has been/is being/will be consumed. The armies formed out of bits of Orphanarium. The armies formed out of the bones of its children.

The church bursts open and finds itself flooded with swarms of apocalyptic beasts fulfilling apocalyptic visions.

THE SECOND DEATH OF CYBERIA CHAPTER

The suns in the church flicker and go out. The screens dissolve. The sand continues to seep in. There is a small glow of light around us, the mind monitors of the two Cyberias. Two glowing fists belonging to the Bearded Dragon. Killy is on the ground running circles around us, barks reverberating off the high ceiling. A skeletal cyborg attempts to charge through us but the Bearded Dragon smacks it down, bones splintering, skull cracking, steel armour folding and falling apart.

"Everybody run!" the Bearded Dragon yells.

More shadowed beasts come charging at us, and each time the Bearded Dragon hammers his glowing fists into them and sends them skidding away. In the skirmish, I am separated from you and Cyberia and Killy, the Bearded Dragon. The clone Cyberia is here with me. We try to keep together, to work our way back to you, but the rush of bodies between us, the rush of things tearing this church apart is impossible to breach. The lightning flash of blades splitting things into perfect pieces, the Chameleon protecting us.

And Killy seems to pass between the two Cyberias. She knows the difference between the two—when you've been through what we have together, you can just tell these things—but it doesn't seem to matter to her. Fundamentally, in their android cores, they are identical. Copies of each other.

Back when it was just us and the lizards, we had some idea what we were up against. Now, we get visions of your grisly death. We get visions of our home crumbling to pieces. We don't know what we fight for any more. We don't know who we are. I don't know why I was so concerned for you, Dil. While the Chameleon and the Bearded Dragon are fighting our battles for us, a chunk of concrete falls from the ceiling, falling and twisting and falling and transforming and at the point of impact your Cyberia is swallowed by a concrete golem. The walls bend and contort. Killy screams almost to the point of suicide. From the ceiling rains the hot sand of our deserts. Bury the cactus. You and Cyberia and the Bearded Dragon, you are now stolen from my vision, disappeared into a sea of bodies, not floating, drowning.

Other creatures press in from all sides, crushing, suffocating. Even the Chameleon becomes a distant dream. Lights flickering, originating from some body or another. Strange creatures illuminating this space and casting long shadows over the violence.

At some point the church becomes washed through with the rest of the Orphanarium. The boundaries between sectors crumble and slide and settle, forming new barriers. It stretches on for what feels like forever, a mutated landscape, and a prick of cold steel to the chest. Stabbed with some form of sabre or sword. A spine. Plucked from a metallic cactus?

It comes with the familiar sensation of sliding away, somewhere between a memory of mine and an observation. What I see, I'm not sure if it's happening now or if it's stolen from another point in time. Just as your clone Cyberia has died/is dying/will die, our Cyberia of memory, the one which held our hands while we rode the elevator to the World Cactus, she is standing on a platform in the middle of a great, wide room, cold and silent, and something sinister rips at her synthetic flesh, claws ripping and slicing and tearing her into a bloody mess until she becomes limp and lifeless, beheaded tumbling down into an ocean of what, I don't know.

I feel her head tumbling down just as real as with each breath my body shakes and whisper-screams a mantra to take me to other places, anywhere but here.

THE SECRET MEETING OF THE BROTHERS OF MEMORY CHAPTER

What happened back when the Orphanarium was being constructed, before the Orphanarium was a thing. What happened when we were born. What happened yesterday, today, tomorrow. Between now and the end of time. This end or that, does it matter? You were there, I was there. We watched each other die. We watched the sun go out. We waited for it to ignite a trigger of new suns. A chain reaction. A blinding light.

The founding members of the the Brothers of Memory. The first meeting. Your church, your legacy. You saw it all come together. You saw it all fall apart. You witnessed everything from the time capsule you call a brain. Your self-induced coma. Like your obsession with the war you played out in your mind over and over again, you looped yourself upwards into infinity. Detached from one brother and latched on to thousands of symbolic others.

I am standing outside your home. I am wondering why, after all this time, you invited me here. And then I open the door to this tormented fragment of your life. What has since become a flickering dream, like objects rushing past you while you're looking out the window of a speeding train. You can't hold on to it. That which is already gone. The mystery has become your new identity. The splitting of images, people into other selves. Same, but different. Unlocking the secrets that exist beneath your skin. The secrets in your flesh. Yeah, *Cyberia* was the cactus junkie...

You're hanging up on that wall again, still, forever you hang. So pale you look like death. And why you wanted us to see you like this, I don't know. Why you brought us down here, why you created your empire out of spines and screens, harnessed images and memories, prophecies, why you couldn't see anything any more but apocalypse. Everything around you becoming the dream of chaos, the delirium of limbs being torn off, guts being split open and organs popped like balloons. The walls around you crumbling.

With that many spines sticking in you, who knows what's real any more?

CHAPTER OF THE BROKEN BIRTHING MACHINE AND THE CRUMBLING CHURCH

Who am I, Dil? Who am I? What's my name? Speak to me. Tell me the things you know. Tell me what you know. Tell me the things you know I know. Tell me how you know me. How you know all about the things we did while we were growing up. How you remember them and cherish them and hold them dear in your memory. How nothing will ever let you forget them.

You remember Cyberia. You remember her, right? And Killy? Our pet cyborg dog who was born out of the air like you and me, but has since been built up with robot parts so she can live longer. You remember riding the elevator? You remember the World Cactus? You remember the dreams, the unreal experience, transcending space beyond the here and now?

We were immortal.

At the start of us, there was a soft blue tinting in the air, the birthing machine creating us in the space of the room and sending us out into the world. This is how we are born in the Orphanarium. We step out. The first Elemental we know is our mother.

And she is dying.

And everything you ever loved is dead or dying.

And everything you ever built is crumbling. So suddenly it is becoming forgotten. Buried.

This is your mother. Look at her and remember. This is who you are. Where you came from. Where you return. She is all machine and she is the mother of orphans. The mother of us. Yes, there is not much left of her. There is not much left of anything any more. Such is the light of this world fading. The heat of its core radiating outward, preparing to end itself and transform into something much younger.

This is your mother.

Look at her.

THE THIRD VISION CHAPTER

You have a spine for everything. Truly, you do. You have a spine, you have an answer. You don't need to know me. You don't need to remember. Because you already forgot. Because the spines show you everything you need to know. Riding out your life one dream to the next to the next.

And the terrifying thing is that I can't fill the blanks in for you any more. I can't remember everything any more. I don't remember how we got here. How we reached this image of you up high with countless needles sticking through every part of you.

The plant-men rolled into one giant beast. A harvest of a particularly potent cactus, spines like we've never seen before.

When you're dead and dreaming, a million visions rolled into one, your cyborg lizard friends, the Bearded Dragon and the Chameleon, they turn against me. For the moment, all the monsters and orphans and Elementals are populating other parts of this world. It is just us. Returned to the room where Cyberia was sliced so thin and head rolled off. Her mind monitor still flickering and displaying alien images.

A spine sticking from her neck.

Return to the image of the Orphanarium becoming detached from its foundations, growing more detached still. The cracks and holes of it becoming sealed back up from the inside. The furiously decaying Elementals trapped outside go crazy trying to bash their way inside. Those left behind. Those who came too late. And everything else is sinking and disappearing. The cities sinking, forests and mountains sinking. Vanishing Mountain sliding into eternal nothing, its moonlit path being swallowed all the way up.

We are not long left for this world.

A burst of bright light from the Chameleon sears past my face, blistering. I duck and dodge the lasers. And the big swinging fists of the Bearded Dragon, I avoid them too. The blades these monsters swing. I scramble backwards and run. I time my movements to coincide with theirs.

In the running, I feel glass discs beneath my feet. I tumble and roll and pick one up. As the Chameleon fires his laser, it becomes reflected off the disc and cuts into the Bearded Dragon. A part of his torso falls off, a large chunk. Part of his face is melted and part of his fist has been obliterated. Another blast of light reflecting back on the Chameleon, his laser canon exploding to pieces, burning his arm, his neck, part of his chest. He rushes at me with a blade extended and leaps on top of me, crushing me beneath his weight.

This is the adrenaline sensation of being alive another moment.

The pain of raw skin tearing and bones popping, snapping.

Except they don't.

He stabs at my face and peels open part of my radioactive skull. I snap his hand off at the wrist, blade tumbling aside, and with my weight kick him off me and proceed to smash him to pieces.

With a rage-howl from the Bearded Dragon, he charges at me too. He will put my bones to the test. And in my head, through the pulsing and aching, I curse everything I know for putting me in this situation. I curse the orphans and the Elementals. I curse the Orphanarium and the outside world. I curse the earth and the sky, the space and the Sky Jaws. I curse you and Cyberia and Killy. I curse myself for the death that I've done. I curse myself in unforgettable ways and I rise to face the Bearded Dragon, the blood of his brother dripping from my body.

As much as I don't know you, brother, I don't even really know myself.

FINAL SUNBURST CHAPTER
(AKA LOVE SONG AND DEATH DANCE)

I don't remember killing the Bearded Dragon, but I've heard it happened. I heard it was true. And I heard it was ugly for both of us. I can feel my half of it. With every step, a limp, I can feel it.

And I can feel the nightmares of this world lifting. This whole world lifting and becoming something else. Whatever the war, there will always be a new balance at the end of it. Cyberia's screen has stopped broadcasting images. I know there is no bringing her back from this one. There is no bringing you back either. I don't know where Killy is, but if she is somewhere out there still fighting against her fear, she will find her way back home.

Just as this place has died/is dying/will die, all I can do is continue to exist until some day I don't.

And Sunburst explodes from the wall and grabs my hand in her hot hand and brings me running through another wall, a molten curtain through which we both pass unharmed, into the new Castle Nothing in the restructured Orphanarium.

"I thought you might like to see this," she says.

You are gone, brother, lost in your memory and bloodless-cold body, hanging forever in the Orphanarium forever hanging, lost to me, to Cyberia, to yourself.

Here in Castle Nothing sits your deathly body, the perfect image of you smiling strangely at me like your mind is vacant of all its memories. You, my brother, your clone an empty vessel waiting to be taught everything it needs to know.

One day it will know the things you know and you will once again be alive as you are.

"It's the least I could do," Sunburst says. "I've been following you."
     I nod. I love her.

Sunburst, I love you.

She leaves me with your clone to fill with memories. No spines. Actual memories.

CHAPTER OF DISINTEGRATION, EXPOSURE OF THE GLASS PLANET, AND SENDING THE ORPHANARIUM INTO SPACE FOREVER

This is how it all ends.

This is you, my brother. Lost and found. Not quite there. Hanging in the liminal space between nothing and everything. Hanging here silently watching, patiently listening.

Where do we go from here? What do we do now?

This is still a world of ruin. This is still a world in collapse.

I'm sick of visions, memories, dreams induced by other powers. I'm sick of playing with hyper-realities. I'm sick of drowning in an ocean of I don't know what.

The Orphanarium has held/is holding/will hold together. The world has broken/is breaking/will break apart.

My one remaining memento, that first spine where I fell in love with Sunburst, is now discarded through a high up window in Castle Nothing, disappears into the void.

We find ourselves in an outer room of the Orphanarium. A space where no one goes. There is a thick plate of glass between us and the world outside. My hand on the glass and the hand of your clone, identical.

I miss you. I miss Cyberia. Killy still hasn't returned. I love your clone with all my heart, and yet I know he is not the same as you. He did not kill the Janken Brothers with us. That was you. Is you. Will forever be you.

This book is full of variables. Some things we know. Some things we don't know. Some things we're going to find out when the time is right. Some of it just comes down to how well we know the details. How we process the information.
Here I am. I am here in the Orphanarium. A city in a massive box. Vacuum sealed tight like no one would be allowed outside. No one is allowed outside. Here, people are born out of the air or made like computers and put together. Outside, the world is disintegrating. Everything reduced to red desert sand and sliding off the planet. We are off the planet and drifting. Pulling out into space. We are a satellite floating through space forever. The sand falls off the bottom of the planet and spirals into space like it's going down a giant cosmic drain. And the core of the planet is small and bright. A sun contained within a glass sphere.

As everything forever has died/is dying/will die, we float on towards our inevitable apocalypse and know there is no stopping it.

OVERGROWN

In the forests we learned to run, in a world much larger than ourselves, and we felt so free while doing it. When we stopped, we had no idea where we were or what we were doing. We sat inside this husk of one thing once living, now dead. A giant beast we can't imagine because it was much bigger when it was alive and our imaginations don't stretch that far.

We are six billion years away from anything. Past and future. In the present, so far away. If we were to go six billion years, we would still be exactly that far away from anything. I guess that's what you'd call infinite. That's our number.

We have no home, yet everywhere seems like home. What we find is all that we already own. What we see, what we feel in the air and beneath our horned feet and rippling over our thick skin. All of this is ours for the finding, keeping, burning into oblivion, should we want the heat of the fire to be ours. Should we want the glow to be burned into our eyes for future remembering.

We play games in the spaces of our world as we pass through them. We count the dead ones sewn into the ground. We count the dead ones grown into the walls, and the ones suspended from the ceiling. They hang like angels and when the wind sways their bodies it sweeps the dust gently off them and brings it down to us like snow.

We count the suns in the rooms we pass, both the dead ones and the ones still burning. How could we not? This is our game, and we own it. We wipe the dust from our masks and we keep counting. We count and keep records in our memory.

Occasionally we find loose skulls to store things in. We tie string through their eye holes and wear them around our necks. The more of them we collect, they jangle as we walk, hollow instruments playing their random toccata and fugues. We call them the doom skulls, and when they have finished their song, when our necks become overburdened with their number, we release them and begin again. We leave them hanging from trees. We leave them for the wind to play with, to encounter the chance of song played by the hands of another composer. We leave them behind and keep counting upwards to six billion.

Everywhere we go is forest. Is jungle. Is dust and decay. Everywhere we go, dead things overgrown with the others we don't know if they're dead or alive.

A giant face on the wall, almost a sculpture, almost humming with life, a portrait of the way things were, preserved forever. Sometimes the trees climbing from the ground or walls or ceiling seem much too real to be trees. The limbs more like creature limbs. Arms with shoulders and elbows and digits on the end of hands. These ones that bend and wave like they're communicating with us. When we see them we leave. We don't linger. We don't try to understand them. We definitely don't try to burn them because we don't know what we would do should they start to scream.

Ours is the only voice in this world, and it goes unused. There is no need, when other voices are held so far away by creatures unimagined. What would we do, should we hear a response? What would we do, should we discover that this world we own may not be entirely ours?

The room we are in begins to crumble. The cords suspending the dead ones snap and one by one the dead ones fall. They become unstuck from the wall and tumble down. They fall from such a great height that some of them splatter. Chunks of what they used to be. The self rendered oblivion by hard ground.

In this room, chunks of ceiling fall down with the dead ones. We run. As we run, we watch the things falling, the holes in the ceiling counted upwards to our number, and behind the ceiling is more forest, more jungle, more decaying world and dead ones. Nothing hits us, but it hurts us so. We witness our own world falling apart and we are helpless to protect it, to preserve it.

The numbers are changing. Suns go out as we count them. We can't go chasing these numbers.

The tree limbs reach out to us, fingers grasping like no tree ever should. We try to count the limbs around us which go against the way of the trees, but their number as we run becomes too difficult to count. One trips us up and we slam on concrete and tree roots. Our mouth meets blood. Our head meets loud static, numbers coming loose, jumbled, a machine blending them into chaos. When we kick free of the damned limb which tripped us, we rise to find that not everything is dead.

Some of the dead ones survived the fall. Some of them are badly broken, crumbled stone-like pieces of them fallen apart, yet whole enough to stand up and shake off all the excess dust. They tower over us. They tower over the trees and they look lost, sad. Like the world around them dissolved in an instant and they do not yet know where they are now.

One of them plucks a low-hanging sun from the air and holds the burning sphere in its hands. The others flock to it, a little wonder for them all to cherish. The creature with the sun holds it close, tight, keeping the light from escaping too far, protecting it from the others. As more of them crowd in, they begin to push and shove.

The sun spills free and comes crashing down, setting the forest on fire. This fire which is more than just a number. They brawl. They jump and tackle. They punch and push and rip each other apart.

We are once again pulled to the ground by frantic limbs. This time more than one. This time they wrap themselves around us and pull us sinking into the ground, into darkness where the fire can't reach. Where the giant creatures can't hurt us. We are damp and cold and our numbers are lost.

There is no pattern for counting chaos.

Our body aching, our moment wrapped in the living limbs of things imitating trees and pulling us through solid ground, the darkness slips through us like an ocean passing through a sponge. By the time we realise we're free falling, there's nothing to hold on to. There's only the gravity song of wind rushing past our ears. The rise of gooseflesh on our arms and legs, our chest. We fall into the nothing space, a place outside the rooms which constitute our world. We are spiralling. Our eyes are bursting with the absolute night surrounding us. And then it becomes apparent that the colours burning into our vision aren't imagined. They're the stars from space. The stuff we've seen painted on walls or drawn in books. Prophecies of the great beyond. Theories that they consist of matter from which we were all born, and what we all are inevitably reduced to. Stars.

At the same time, they seem so cold and distant, yet so warm and real. A part of ourselves we wish to embrace so completely. Our fall into space comes to an end when we plummet into the cold ocean and ripple the image of stars around us, blurring the image as we look up through watery lenses.

This space which seemed so dark becomes a bloom of night light. Crawling and twinkling with gentle light rippling on the water's surface. The water itself becomes illuminated and a giant face comes into view. It is cool and white and smooth. One of the many mechanical creatures which was long dead before we came into this world. It haunts the ocean floor with its steel glow, while another creature breaks the surface of the water, its bright white face resembling so many others, winding towards us on a serpentine neck while its body remains submerged. It stares at us like a puzzle, peering from different angles to gauge why we're here in this ocean. It needs no words to communicate with us. It needs no words to read us for who we are.

What we want is to live with some semblance of truth.

We wish only to understand the world in which we exist.

We wish only to know this world for what it is. What our role is within it. What has changed this world from a place of dead ones to something more organic, something which is not finished dying.

We float and wonder how much information the long-necked ocean creature wishes to extract from us. We think of what it knows about us just from looking. Our history. Our thoughts. Our emotions. What this creature is capable of knowing, what it is capable of doing.

Life in this world is a mystery to us. All we know is dead things. Even now we don't really know that any more. The ocean creature's torso rises above the water, its exoskeleton shining bright in the starlight. An arm telescopes out towards us, a hand extended (a hand not unlike our own) touches us, and we begin to glow white. A beacon floating in the dark water.

We are lit up like this ocean creature just turned us on. It reels its hand back in and sinks beneath the surface, its neck winding back down, a disappearing face the last to go. It leaves us wondering if the giant face on the ocean floor is alive too. What else in this world may have come alive. What else swims in these waters. What madness has disrupted our serenity.

Far above us, there have appeared a series of big ships moving overhead on thick steel cables moving overhead. Blue lights blinking their position, shining the grey steel and red rust of them.

The miracle of the ships and cables is that they do not once obscure the line of sight of the stars. One pauses above us and opens a mouth on its underside, a mechanical claw winding down, lights pulsing, an alien enigma. The claw moves curiously, like the face of the ocean creature exploring us before it. We are seized in its pincers, held in it like a cradle, robot fingers. The machine pulls us up and out of the water towards the ship's gaping maw. We are drawn into it and from inside is all transparent looking out, the twinkling stars on the walls move as the ship resumes its voyage.

We never imagined we would glimpse this much space in our lifetimes. We never imagined we would ride on board a cable-driven space ship. Everything we knew becomes unravelled. A snake emerging from a black hole which seems to be forever emerging, expanding, forever repeating its length out into the universe. Pulling on its tail amounts to nothing but more length of it to pull. We are two hands, all thumbs, lost in space without so much as a number to keep the calm. No order to speak of. Every memory accounted for. Memories of an intangible past so swiftly made redundant. Memories for the black hole.

The ship we're in is one of a fleet of hundreds, thousands,

millions. We see them here in this space, as we saw their dead brothers and sisters hanging disused in the rooms of our world. The old dead ships which may have resumed their journeys as these ships have done. A journey into what? There is no pilot to this ship. No controls except the push and pull of cables above us. The gentle swing in the night breeze.

The haunting face in the ocean far below us, still gracefully glowing its nothing face up at us. The creatures swimming in the ocean. Tiny creatures on the ship, humanoid aliens with pale dome heads, too many limbs and far, far too many teeth. We sit amongst them and draw no attention to ourselves. We follow the image of the cable along which we crawl. Pulling towards the stars on one wall. We see the stars as carefully projected image the moment the wall hinges open to let the ship pull through. This is when we notice the twinkling stars for what they really are—the hinging open and closed twinkle of light from another place, another space in this cosmic building-world. A complex cube hurtling through space far faster than we would care to calculate.

A soft blue light combs through our hair as the breeze ripples through the ship. At first light the tiny creatures ripple panic across our skin and disappear in the folds of the ship. We pass over an ocean which is a far truer colour of the world we know. It lays flat like glass and refuses to move, yet there are bodies beneath it, some still, some moving, some trying to break the surface and float into the air. None of them do.

Our ship tracks on, and the hundreds of other ships around us, above and below, now steel grey in the new light, more solid, more real, move in all directions. An armada of chaos. A fleet moving by direction of random chance. We are segmented into two colonies: the ships and the underwater ones. Everything appearing as the image of clarity, yet so unreal, so much of skimming the surface and no full immersion. No plunge into the deep well of understanding, the worlds of us just as foreign as the worlds of others.

We stare into the faces of the unknown drowned ones and we are agitated at the thought that we can do nothing. They are trapped beneath glass. We hear them tapping and their rhythm becomes our irregular heart beat. We wait for the inevitable cracking of the glass, yet we figure we may be waiting days or months or years.

The breeze surrounding us transforms into a vortex, pulling the ship around us into nothing. The little creatures drop like bombs and explode—like bombs—all around us on the glass below. Nothing penetrates the surface. Where there is nothing beneath us, where we should plummet, we drift like an invisible parachute guides us down. Where we land on the glass, there is a menacing lizard face frozen under our feet. Deep growls, and a wild heat radiating from it. Alive in its eyes. Before our feet burn and sink into melted glass, we run.

The sky is lit up with thousands of burning little creatures, falling and exploding and turning into ash. Little explosions, a whoosh of air, a resultant cloud of change. Kamikaze creatures raining down. Giant lizard monsters burning their way up.

Whirring computers from other places break the glass into neat platforms, sending them up in the air. We are hovering on transparent spaces. The beasts in the ocean are liberated. The lizard bursts its flaming head from the waves, expands its wings metallic, somewhat cyborgean, and twists between platforms, soaring into the sky.

Above the platforms, the cables driving the ships remain, obstacles for the beast. From the ocean comes smaller beasts.

Machines with whirring blades cutting through the water and turning it to foam. Cutting through glass and reducing it to shards. Moving so fast that the death of everything around them seems like an inevitability.

Creatures of the sea machines dip in and out of the water, plastic human faces opening their modest mouths to reveal dystopian jaws to crush the blade beasts.

Each monster seems more destructive or more gigantic than the last.

Each monster seems totally oblivious towards the concept of annihilation.

We run from platform to platform. We leap and hope that what we land on is glass and not an optical illusion which will send us plummeting to the ocean. A straight drop down into the compound jaws of some humanesque monster mimicking our face and churning us into food.

We imagine a misinterpreted jump, flipping and landing on another platform, hitting the corner of it on the small of our back. A heavy crack, and life as we know it ends right there. We imagine falling after the fact. The twisting and contorting, the uselessness of our own limbs. The knowledge that we will hit every other platform on the way down, falling and smacking and breaking, falling like a ragdoll until we come to a rest, useless and dying while monsters and machines ravenously pull each other apart around us.

An entire wall is torn down from the outside. A giant humanoid robot bursting its way into combat. In its chest is a giant sphere of light and concentric rings. The rings begin to spin upon themselves, gaining speed until some seem to spin in reverse while others appear to be suspended, hanging still. The hypnosis of this device provides the sensation that our feet are no longer planted on firm glass. We drift, along with the monsters, machines, platforms and ocean, into suspended space, more towards the ceiling than the ground.

We use our space to bounce off platforms, pushing from one to another to escape the fate of dying before we fully know what this world is which we're in.

Everything bleeds between liminal spaces.

Everything folds upon itself.

Everything burns and collapses and bursts forth from nothing.

What sounds we make, as beasts communicating with other beasts, the response we get is either confusion or indifference. We say more with our body language than we do with our words. In the skirmish, all the other monsters are lost to the power of this demonic android pulling us free of our gravity. We share our collective with the monsters and machines around us in that we are all of us lost and floating and struggling to hold on to something.

The weapons of those other beasts still rip and slice and explode, but they too lose control as we lose control.

We can't keep leaping across platforms. We reach out to the others and they float on by. We are drenched in pieces of ocean. We want to understand at least something before we die. We want not to drown like this. Distorted image of the giant android with his trembling, spinning, gravity-blending sphere. Image photographed in our lenses forever.

The things we could show you if you had our eyes.

Amongst us there are plenty of dead things floating around. Biological things. Indestructible things. Destroyed. Obliterated. Things which once had names but are now nameless.

The walls break apart and their debris becomes part of the floating mass, the chaos of our new world reconstructing itself. A wingless lizard machine comes through the open space and blasts through the debris of us and them. Its shell is glass and inside it are dozens of small cyborgs, each glowing with their own colour, making up rainbows in the creature's shell, transmitting the rainbows out and using the light to cut through the air like a guillotine.

Its arms are twin soldiers—blade and shield a part of each other—and this massive glowing creature howls into the air, freezing our gravity where it hangs, and sending the suns into darkness. Its painted glow floods the darkness as the shimmering orb of the menacing android becomes still, silent, dark. The lizard cyborg opens its mouth again and blasts a cosmic beam, a trail of pure golden light, straight into the android's sphere, its core obliterated into nothing.

We are all brushed aside so the lizard cyborg can approach the android poised still at the other end of the room.

The giant lizard, so bright, so full of light and life—the life of galaxies within him—he charges at the android like a kinetic virus has rusted itself to his silicon bones.

He charges with shield-arm raised and blade coiled back—a gun ready to fire—to stab and spill robot guts into the vacant space of what was once ocean. The android clicks and hums when the lizard is three steps away. He raises an arm to block the shield and avoid the blade. It slashes air. The lizard crashes past, a twisted dance, and the android fires up its jet-pack feet and turns around to face its attacker, its body twisting in inhuman ways. Its face repositioned like a rubik's puzzle distorted then once again made complete.

We gaze through the broken wall like a cinema screen, the battle spilled out into the other room. None of the other creatures in here have resumed their war. None of them seem to know what to make of it. Staring through the broken walls into the other spaces, it reveals to us that combat is the new world order. Stars colliding and burning into new things, the explosions forming everything we know and have ever known, the number of everything in between now and then, the number of everything vast beyond, the number of our universe stretching out infinite, a spectrum of everything beyond us unattainable, what we know is that the order of things have come to this, and through each broken down wall, there is some giant beast or other ripping and smashing and attempting to destroy another.

They try to ensure their mutual destruction. They bathe in each other's machine-gore.

Lights flashing and machines grinding otherworldly orchestras. The forests of what once was, they rain down through the ceiling. They rain from the walls and the floor. Everything pulling apart and floating between rooms. The forests of trees with much more life than what should be, they form chains of limbs holding on to each other, forming ropes with which to catch this world, to hold it together or to trap it and begin the greater forest over again.

Through the walls, the lizard and the android, floating and fighting, blasting and slicing and stabbing, splitting each other open, smashing cavities, shattered oblivion, they crash back into our space, returning to us and the half-dozen other giant, fighting beasts.

The lizard slices the android's torso in two with his blade now glowing red hot and covered in grease-blood. The android body crashes to its knees, falling past where the ocean used to be and sprawling out on what is left of the actual ground.

The other giants continue brawling. The room becomes infected with a fine red mist. The blood of dead ones—big and small—mixed with the ocean pulled into clouds from the gravity come apart.

We hover in this space, and the lizard victor turns back this way and slashes through the air. Through the red mist, its kaleidoscopic form comes this way. Its crystal blade slashes through the red. It smashes glass. The smaller beings in the air become bisected or are cut up into oblivion. The lizard carves its way across the room, and so fine are its sword strokes, it will be upon its next big enemy in no time. It will breeze past us and either destroy us or leave us, indifferent to our existence in this world.

There is not much left of this structure which could be called a room any more. The walls which contain us are concentric walls to the ones we had before, much bigger, much further beyond us. The night room bleeds into ours, and from it, the ocean monsters crawl out and present their silicon-white faces as puzzles, mysteries detecting mysteries. The giant face on the bottom of the ocean, it has been liberated too, come alive, joined the frenetic dance of living things left in this world.

Is this a revolution of things beginning again? Or is this the chaos dance of one last fling before the lights go out?

All the faces, all the twisted bodies, grotesque machines and monsters, cyborgs, androids, giant species existing in combination with all of the above. What will remain of this world when we draw our final breath? What will we have learned? What accomplishments will mark its record of our time within this universe? Almost nothing.

As the slashing blade draws closer, we know it will hit us. We can do nothing to avoid it. As it draws closer, we see the intricacies of its design. The intricacies of its movement. The long blade, razor sharp edge, blood gutter running down its length. It slashes, it cuts, blood glistening on its crystal surface. Sometimes, however, it swings on its flat edge. Not cutting, but pushing. Choosing its victims much more intricately than thought possible of a large, violent beast.

We are swept up on the side of the blade. We slide into the blood gutter and we slide with other creatures down the length of the blade. We are caught up in its narrow passage, disappearing through a hole into the lizard's body with the cyborgs, floating, with all the new creatures, becoming part of this living organism.

We wish to know the mysteries of the universe, to know the unknowable. Like understanding the creatures once living now dead, and the creatures once dead now living.

We wish to know the creatures eternal, woven into the history of the universe, stretching and spiralling out in numbers unimaginable, mutating and evolving into larger and more complex creatures and becoming entirely new things as they continue on in their existence.

We wish to know this world we're in, what's holding it together and what's tearing it apart. What the cause was for its death, hurtling through space, its life so long ago, what creatures existed within it back then, what magic compelled it, and if that magic still exists now, and if so how, and if those old creatures were the same as the ones that are here now, like the one which caught me inside its transparent body, if they are the creatures, are they the same, or are they modified versions, what compels them to destroy or protect, what compels them to come alive and act upon unknown impulses.

We are carried on in its body, a series of footholds and handholds, rungs on the inside of its body, across which we climb to anchor ourselves in the best spot to watch the giant lizard attack the silicon warrior from the deep.

From within, everything is amplified. The sound, the feeling, the movement, the crystal clarity of everything ahead of us. Charging into battle against a great ugly demon. Flashing lights and otherworldly noises. The delicate web of life which previously sustained balance in this world come undone, shaken loose by what we can only imagine as an upset giant child-like creature, shaking the threads loose as its face contorts into a howl.

Violent is the nature of the act. The disruption jolts us from our senses, our old body morphed into this heightened plane of awareness. Everything around us is precious. A memory for the vault. Everything seeming too fragile, with lifespans far too short for this once-eternal world, and now it seems obscene to reduce the items and bodies and beings around us to numbers. They are archives, histories, lost or fleeting from this world.

How much longer the outer walls can hold together, we don't know. How long before the beasts within this vessel tear it to the point of disintegration, we don't know.

The crystal-glass lizard creature continues to devastate those around him. He thrashes and shoves, he throws laser beams right through walls into cold beasts. He twists in the air and stabs. He is in control, yet how much of the control comes from within? Burning. The world flickers blue-red, then orange and black. Someone has lit the world on fire, and slowly it is being consumed.

The beast of it becoming fuel for the dead.

Melted rubber, burnt wood, scorched steel. Carbon and silicon. Silver and bone.

The cyborgs within the lizard panic. The lizard panics. He hurtles through space. He smashes against wall or ceiling or floor. He shatters. Everything around us shatters and the heat of the fire gets in our skin. Smashing and burning and floating with all the dead things.

We are wrapped up in our own little world. We are combined with self-destruction, annihilation, apocalypse. These are the words of us. These are the words of our people. The language of setting yourself of fire. The burial of your newborn sons. The love your life will never guarantee. The rapid expansion of your universe as it consumes everything around you. The moment when you realise your entire existence is defined by everyday ghosts. The time you remembered just exactly who you were and exactly what you were doing in this world. The time when you had meaning beyond existence. The space you had, your physical body had a sense of belonging. There was no being pulled along. There was no coming and going with the tide. There was no drifting or floating. There was only you. And now there is only us. Only the casual drift towards nothing. The numbers rewritten, erased.

We were here only to live, to catalogue in our own memory vaults the world preserved, retained and floating through space, an enigma to project the mystery of universes.

We unravelled our worlds and became what we saw.

We absorbed them and wished them not to be disturbed.

We tried so hard to keep this world sacred, to use these hands to hold it together, to keep it in tact, to protect it from all that ever was and all that ever will be. But that was not our purpose nor our strength. It was an ambition far exceeding its practical application.

We fell apart. We snapped. We became unwound by space. We were torn to pieces by the will of the universe.

Our home became a thing of fragments, drifting apart.

We became overburdened by this world too overgrown. Its life far exceeding our own. Its life an ambitious project by some immaculate god or machine. Its existence so thorough and complex and violent, yet so rich and beautiful and beyond reach.

We can not calculate the number of creatures who fought to be here. We can not find all the pieces, the earth and concrete, drifting apart.

Everything around us drifts apart as we float in pieces, as we too drift apart. We have come undone as our world has come undone.

ABOUT THE AUTHOR

S.T. Cartledge is a bizarro fiction author and poet based in Perth, Western Australia. This is his fifth book, and his first full-length foray into sci-fi inspired surrealism. His novelette, *Wizard and Robot in the World of Sand and Bones* and his forthcoming novella, *Girl in the Glass Planet* (Bizarro Pulp Press, 2017) continue to explore these otherworldly dreamscapes.